Praise from the U.K. for
Charles Webb's
NEW CARDIFF

"Brilliantly funny . . . Webb writes with a kind of disciplined and suppressed joy in his creations, and this joy quickly transfers itself to the reader. Anyone who manages to resist the charm of these quirky and tangential relationships should be regarded with deep suspicion. . . . Effortlessly delightful."

—Nick Hornby, *The Sunday Times* (U.K.)

"Charming . . . It is almost all dialogue, dialogue of such natural-ic pithiness that one seems to hear it in the mind's ear . . . cloyingly romantic and witty."

—*The Spectator*

"is rare to come across something done with so light a touch such precision. This slim, deadpan novel isn't carrying an nce of fat. . . . Webb has something like the comic equivalent perfect pitch."

—*Literary Review*

"uated in a tradition spanning Henry James to *Notting Hill*. . . . ere is a pared-down simplicity to the novel . . . of a fairy tale or perhaps a m . . . funny."

Also by Charles Webb

The Graduate
Love, Roger
The Marriage of a Young Stockbroker
Orphans & Other Children
The Abolitionist of Clark Gable Place
Elsinor
Booze

New Cardiff

Charles Webb

WASHINGTON SQUARE PRESS
PUBLISHED BY POCKET BOOKS

New York   London   Toronto   Sydney   Singapore

This book is a work of fiction. Names, characters, places and incidents are products of the author's imagination or are used fictitiously. Any resemblance to actual events or locales or persons, living or dead, is entirely coincidental.

 WSP

A Washington Square Press Publication of
POCKET BOOKS, a division of Simon & Schuster, Inc.
1230 Avenue of the Americas, New York, NY 10020

Copyright © 2001 by Charles Webb

Originally published in Great Britain in 2001 by Little, Brown and Company

Published by arrangement with Little, Brown and Company

ISBN: 0-7434-4416-7

First Washington Square Press trade paperback printing January 2002

10 9 8 7 6 5 4 3 2 1

WASHINGTON SQUARE PRESS and colophon are registered trademarks of Simon & Schuster, Inc.

For information regarding special discounts for bulk purchases,
please contact Simon & Schuster Special Sales at 1-800-456-6798
or business@simonandschuster.com

Every effort has been made to trace the copyright holders for 'A Woman's Heart' by Eleanor McEvoy. If notified, the publisher will be pleased to rectify any omission in future editions.

Illustrations by Fred

Cover design by Regina Starace
Cover photos: (figure) © Tim MacPherson/Stone; (leaf and suitcase) © PhotoDisc

Printed in the U.S.A.

For David Gritten,
who dropped everything to research the origin of
'hat trick', and do whatever else was necessary
to make us at home in the realm.

And Caroline Dawnay,
whose warmth, generosity and humour
typify what we've found to be the British spirit.

Without the patient, skilful and affectionate
editorial guidance of Philippa Harrison
this novel would have stopped well short of its destination.

Part I

1

Colin was standing in front of the art supply store when it opened at nine o'clock, and raised his hand slightly in greeting as a woman walked toward him on the other side of its glass door. He watched as she unlocked it, then as she walked back the way she had come he pushed it open and went inside.

The woman stepped behind a counter and began transferring money from a cloth bag into the drawer of a cash register. She glanced up at Colin, but continued thumbing through the small stacks of bills as she placed them in the drawer.

'I'll just take a look round then,' Colin said, 'if I may.'

It was a small store, but its shelves were crowded with paint brushes, tubes of paint, pads of paper and other artists' materials. Colin walked along one of the short aisles, turned around the end to the next one, then stopped at a display of wooden pencils. He was about to pick one up when he noticed a heavyset man standing in a doorway at the end of the aisle, his arms folded over his chest as he watched Colin. 'Yes,' Colin said, 'I think I've found one of the things I'm looking for.' He turned his attention back to the shelf. 'I don't know if these are designated the same way they are in the UK,' he said, picking up several pencils to examine. 'The way they're numbered according to lead size.' He studied the lettering on the side of one of the pencils, then held it up. 'You don't happen to know if the numbering system for pencils is universal, do you.'

The man hadn't moved or lowered his arms from across his chest. 'I would have no way of knowing that, sir.'

'No,' Colin said. 'Well, it looks like it might be.' He nodded. 'I think I'll assume it is.' He returned a pencil to its compartment on the shelf, then removed one from the next compartment, found the number on it, then selected several more. 'These should get me started.' He looked back at the man. 'Do you sell paper in individual sheets or just in the pads.'

The man was holding one of his hands out to Colin.

'What.'

'I'll hang on to those as you look around.'

'The pencils?'

He nodded.

'That's all right.'

The man's fingers began to flutter slightly.

Colin watched them a moment, then handed him the pencils. 'Well. That's very kind, thank you.'

The man enclosed them in his hand. It was quiet as they looked at each other.

'Twenty-four hours ago,' Colin said finally, 'I had no idea I'd be standing here in America at this time. Yesterday morning, if you'd told me I'd be in the state of Vermont, buying pencils today, I'd have said you were out of your mind.' The man continued to return his gaze. 'But here I am.' Colin looked down at the floor. 'Standing in America.' Again it was quiet for a few moments. 'Buying pencils.'

As Colin walked down to the end of the aisle and around to the next one, the man took a step sideways so he could keep him in sight.

'Here are the pads.' Colin bent forward to pick up a pad of sketch paper from a shelf. 'Do you sell paper by the individual sheet?'

'No.'

'That's all right, this'll do.' He studied the printing on the cover of the pad for a few moments. 'I'm not finding anything about acid content on here,' he said, looking up.

'I didn't hear you,' the man said.

'I need acid-free paper. I don't see anything on the label to tell me whether this is or not.'

'It is,' the man said.

'Acid-free.'

He nodded.

'Because that's fairly important, and it usually says on the label.'

'All paper in this country is acid-free,' the man said.

'Really?'

'That's how it goes.'

Colin looked down at the large pad he was holding. 'I guess it's true what they say about the States – how far ahead of us you are.' He carried it to the front and to the counter.

The woman had finished putting the money into the cash register and was seated behind it on a stool.

'May I put the pad down while I find a few other items?'

'Set it right there.'

He put it down on the counter.

'Where are you from,' she said.

'England.'

'Well I could tell that. Where in England.'

'I grew up in London.'

She nodded. Then it was quiet for a few moments till Colin said, 'I'm going to need some sort of a case. Some kind of carrying case for all my things.'

The woman pointed at a rack on one of the walls.

'Of course the ridiculous thing is I've got every one of these things just sitting there back in my flat,' he said, walking across the room. He reached up over an easel to bring a wooden case down from the rack, then opened it to look inside.

'Are you with a group?' the man said.

'No, just myself.' He returned the case and brought down another.

'Did I hear you say you didn't expect to come over here?' the woman said.

'You did,' Colin said. 'The idea entered my head, I found my passport and an hour later I was on the train to the airport. Two hours after that I was in the air.'

'You're on a personal tour?' the man said.

'I'm not on a tour.'

'He's trying to find out your purpose in being here,' the woman said.

Colin lowered the case to his side. 'Yes,' he said. 'Let me think how to put it. My purpose.'

They waited quietly for him to speak.

'This will sound a bit strange,' he said at last, 'but I'll just say it anyway.' He cleared his throat. 'All right. I read a lot, I always have done, and in a sense that was behind my coming here this way. I'm trying to think how to . . .' Again he cleared his throat. 'I don't know if you're familiar with the tradition in nineteenth-century American fiction – you run across this again and again – where someone will have to get over a love affair of some sort.

Unrequited love, it might be. Or maybe the parents didn't feel their daughter's choice was from the right family, that sort of thing. And actually you find this theme goes right up into the American fiction of the twenties, as I think about it. But in any case, you have the love gone wrong, then off the person gets packed to Europe, on the next ocean liner, to put their relationship behind them. Then around through the different countries they trot, gawking at the castles, canals, ruins and whatnot, till in six months or a year they're ready to sail back to America, broken heart mended, ready to start a new life. At least that was the theory.' He pressed a latch on the case and opened it. 'So I thought I might try it in reverse. I thought I'd see if it would work for me, a hundred years or so later, the other way around.' He closed the case.

The man glanced over at his wife, back at Colin, then again it was quiet in the store.

'A torchon,' Colin said finally. 'Do you carry those?'

'Say it again?' the woman said.

'A torchon.'

'What in hell's that,' the man said.

'Maybe they're not called that here. Let's see, it looks like a pencil, but it's made from tightly rolled paper, and you keep unrolling the end of it to make a point. It's used for blending – pastels usually, but I use it with graphite.'

They kept looking back at him silently.

'I don't think you carry them.'

'Say it once more?' she said.

'Never mind. I can use my thumb.'

She looked at her husband. 'Did Judy used to stock those?'

'Judy never heard of it either.'

'We took the store over from our daughter,' the woman said.

'Don't worry about it – a thumb can do.' Colin carried the case up to put beside the sketch pad on the counter. 'An India rubber.'

'Let's back up here a minute,' the man said, still standing at the end of one of the aisles.

The India rubbers were displayed next to the front counter. Colin began going through them.

'You had a love affair?' the man said.

'A love,' Colin said, holding an India rubber close to his eyes to read the small print on it. 'Or I thought I did. But obviously she didn't share that opinion. Or I wouldn't be here.' He set it down with his other supplies.

'How'd you get here to New Cardiff,' the woman said.

'By bus.'

'You just arrived?'

'Late last night.'

'But not a tour bus.'

'No.'

'Because we get all the coach tours coming through this time of year,' she said, 'with all the beautiful foliage.'

'And it is beautiful,' Colin said.

'Leaf peepers,' the man said from behind him.

'What?' Colin said, turning around.

'Leaf peepers,' he said again.

'Oh.' He nodded, then looked back at the woman. 'I hope I've got enough American money for this.'

'That's all we accept.'

'I know. And I took some out of a cash machine last night at the airport. I may have to ask you to add this up and then I'll find another machine nearby if I don't have quite enough.'

'Give me his pencils.' She held her hand out to her husband.

Colin removed his wallet. 'I think I've got about fifty dollars,' he said, opening it and taking out a bill.

'You can put that one back where it came from,' the man said, stopping next to him and looking down at the bill.

'Oh right,' Colin said. 'Sorry.'

'Can I see that?' The woman held out her hand.

Colin gave it to her. 'It's a ten-pound note.'

'And how much would that be worth.'

Colin shrugged. 'Fourteen dollars or so. I don't really know.' He removed several other bills from his wallet.

'Those are the ones we're looking for,' the man said, nodding at them.

'I know.'

'Here's your queen,' the woman said, studying the note in her hand.

'Yes.'

After looking at it a few more moments, she held it out to show her husband. 'Their queen.'

He nodded, but she continued holding it in front of his face. 'I see it, Martha.' He gestured for her to remove it. 'I see it.'

'I thought you were still looking at her.'

Colin finished counting his American money. 'Forty-eight dollars,' he said. 'With the case that probably won't be quite enough.'

'Why are you in this particular area,' the man said.

'What?'

'That's what I'm not connecting with,' he said, pointing down at the floor. 'Why here.'

'May I ask something about their queen?' the woman said.

'No.'

'That would be all right,' Colin said.

'Whenever I see your queen on the news,' the woman said, 'she always . . .' She shook her head.

'What,' Colin said.

'Her expression,' the woman said. 'I don't know what there is about it.'

'You don't like it?'

'It's not that I don't like it,' she said.

'Well what about it.'

'I'm trying to think how to put it,' she said. 'There's something . . .' Again she shook her head.

'Sort of stiff about it?' Colin said.

'It's not that exactly.'

'Could we worry about this later?' her husband said. 'I'd like the man to tell us why he's in New Cardiff.'

'He doesn't owe you any explanation, Harold.'

'No that's all right,' Colin said. 'It helps me clarify it in my own mind.'

Again they waited for him to speak.

Colin nodded. 'Well of course the region, that was the first decision. East, west – I hadn't even thought about that when I got on. So as we came closer I started thinking . . . you know . . . I'll have to do something, they won't just let me sit on the plane after it lands. New England. I'll go to New England. The name. I mean actually that was the whole reason for the decision. The name.'

'The England part,' the woman said.

'Sort of like a verbal cushion, you might say.'

'You haven't been to our country before,' she said.

'I've always felt I'd come someday.'

'We got you as far as why you picked New England,' the man said. 'Let's keep rolling.'

'Why this particular town?' Colin said. 'Okay. So we landed. The plane landed there in New York. And I got off. I only had hand luggage. And there was a bus that went into the city. I got on that. I got into the terminal in Manhattan. I found another bus, one that was going up through the New England states, and I boarded that one next.' He glanced over at the man. 'I'm reconstructing this.'

'I'm still with you.'

'Okay,' Colin said, 'then there was a woman in the seat next to mine. She got on in New York too, a couple of minutes after I did, sat down next to me, and started talking about her son in the penitentiary.'

'Oh?' the woman said.

'James,' Colin said. 'He's in Sing Sing for thirty-five years.'

'Is that right.'

'Well he's basically a good boy, but apparently his trial wasn't all that fair; some false testimony. She had pictures of him when he was a child, riding in his little cart.' Colin glanced up at the man. 'At one point she asked if I'd come along next time she visited the penitentiary, so James could meet an English person and learn some better manners. She thought this would help him make a more favourable impression at his next parole hearing.'

'Cut to the chase, sir,' the man said. 'Why'd you choose our town.'

'Yes,' Colin said. 'Well it was the monument, to be specific. The bus drove past it. The lights were shining up against it.' He nodded. 'That was the reason.'

'The Battlefield Monument,' the woman said.

'Yes.'

'But what about it.'

'I saw it and I got off.'

'Just because of that?'

'I asked someone on the bus what it was. A Revolutionary War Monument, they said. When the bus stopped I got down my bag and disembarked.'

'And that was the whole reason?'

'I would say it was.'

'But it sounds like that boy's mother was driving you crazy,' the woman said. 'I'm sure you wouldn't have gotten off here if it wasn't for her.'

'I think I would have.'

'Then what,' the man said.

'There were a couple of taxis waiting by the little station. I asked one of the drivers if he knew of a motel. He did. He drove me to one. I checked in.' Colin shrugged. 'And that's it. That's the reason I'm here.'

'Our monument,' the man said.

'Maybe on some level I felt at home knowing some Brits had been here before.'

'And got whupped,' the man said.

'Got what?'

'Got their asses whupped.'

'They lost the battle,' the woman said.

'Oh. Yes. That's true.' Colin nodded. 'But we're all friends now. At least I . . .'

'I'm going to give you a piece of advice,' the man said.

'Okay.'

'Don't visit that woman's son in prison.'

'No.'

'He's in there for a reason.'

'Armed robbery and assault with intent to kill,' Colin said.

'Don't help that bastard get out.'

'Actually I was wondering how realistic it was that a short chat with me would lead to his early release.'

'You let him keep the manners he has,' the woman said.

'I will.'

'If she wanted him to have some manners, the time to teach him those was when she was raising him.'

'Excuse me,' Colin said, frowning slightly, 'I apologise for rushing you, but would you add up the bill? I'm afraid I'm beginning to feel a little faint.'

'Don't faint on us, sir.'

'I'm trying not to.'

'Are you ill?' the woman said.

'Just extremely tired,' Colin said. 'I got no sleep on the plane. Then on the bus I couldn't rest. Then even after I got to the motel room I just seemed to lie there looking up at the ceiling the rest of the night, till the sun came up, then I walked over here.' He looked at his watch. 'And I didn't sleep the night before that either,' he said. 'So it's been about two days.'

'Two days awake?'

'About that.'

'Total him up,' the man said.

The woman began ringing up the items he'd selected on the cash register.

'You're an artist then,' the man said.

'Yes.'

'You should have gotten some coloured pencils so you could draw the foliage.'

'I limit myself to faces.'

'You're not into the landscapes.'

He shook his head. 'Spatial relationships in nature have always defeated me.'

'What sort of faces do you like to draw,' the woman said, as she entered the price of the sketch pad.

'One will strike me. I don't really know why. Like the man at the motel last night. I hadn't thought of doing any drawing over here – that's why I didn't bring my things. Then the man was checking me in and I just felt . . . you know . . . I have to draw this person's face. Of course I don't know if he'll sit for me. I wanted to buy my things first, then ask him when I go back to the motel.'

'Who was it,' the man said.

'Sorry?'

'The man who checked you in.'

'Oh, I don't know his name.'

'What motel was it.'

'I don't even remember that,' he said, opening his wallet. He took out a card to show him.

'That would be Fisher,' the man said, after looking at it.

'Fisher.' Colin nodded and returned the card to his wallet.

'Why would you want to draw Fisher.'

'As I said, there's not really a rational . . .'

'Why would anyone want to draw Fisher,' the man said to his wife. 'The man's face looks like road kill.'

'Don't say that about Fisher, dear.' She tore the receipt off the register and handed it to him. 'That comes to fifty-seven dollars and some change,' she said, 'but I'm going to forget the change because

17

I don't want you to think everybody over here's like the lady you met on the bus.'

'You don't have to do that.'

'I don't want you to think everybody over here's just out for favours for themselves.'

'I know that.'

'Once in a while we like to do something nice for someone else,' she said. 'Americans are very giving people.'

'You're known for your generosity the world over,' Colin said.

'Well I'm so happy to hear you say that. Did you hear that, Harold?'

'Keep the sale moving.'

Colin removed a plastic card from his wallet. 'I'll go to the bank now.'

'And when you get back,' the woman said, 'I'll have everything in a big bag for you.'

'Thank you.' He turned around and went slowly toward the door.

'You don't want a cup of coffee first, do you,' the man said.

'Oh no.'

'We don't want you keeling over before you get the money.'

'You do look a little shaky,' his wife said.

Colin walked the rest of the way across the store. He opened the door, bumping it against his shoe, then moved his foot and pulled it the rest of the way open.

'Can you find the bank?'

'It's in the next street,' he said. 'I saw it earlier.'

'And be very cautious crossing,' the woman said, removing a large plastic bag from under the counter. 'Our traffic goes the opposite way, so be sure and look both left and right before you step off the kerb.'

Colin paused a moment longer in the doorway, then went out into the sunlight. 'I will need to remember that,' he said, 'thank you.'

2

When Colin got back to the motel, Fisher was no longer on duty, and the plaque in the office on which his name had appeared the night before had been replaced by one reading JOANIE FISHER, CO-MGR.

After listening while Colin told her why he wanted to speak to Fisher, the woman explained to him that her husband was driving a table up to their son at his college in New Hampshire, and wouldn't be back till the middle of the afternoon. 'Why would you want to draw Fisher's picture,' she said. 'Not that he isn't a nice-looking man.'

'His bearing struck me,' Colin said.

21

'Oh?'

'But there's really no way to put these things into words,' he said. 'Visual qualities speak for themselves.'

Joanie Fisher was neatening the brochures in a display case against one of the walls of the office. 'I'm sure he'll be very flattered,' she said, 'as far as I know, no one's ever wanted to draw his picture before.'

'I'll try not to take up too much of his time.'

There was a mirror in a ceramic frame next to the door, and as Colin started to leave he caught a glimpse of himself in it and stopped suddenly to look more closely.

Joanie opened a new packet of brochures.

He pushed his hand up the side of his unshaven face. 'God,' he said. He ran his fingers through his hair.

'Something wrong?'

'I haven't given a thought to my appearance in two days.'

'It doesn't really show.'

'It doesn't?'

'We've had worse.'

'Than this?'

'Much.'

'I've never looked worse than this.' He pushed his finger against a puffy fold of darkish skin under his eye. 'Good God.'

'Did you just get in from England?'

'Last night.'

She fitted the new brochures into the case. 'Probably the jet lag.'

Colin continued staring at his face in the mirror.

'We have a friend who travels abroad all the time, and he deals with the jet lag problem by going to bed an hour earlier each night before his trip, so by the time he leaves he's already adjusted to the time difference in the new country.' She stepped back and looked at the case. 'Of course that has its drawbacks too. Last year he had to go to India and by the time he left he was going to bed at ten-thirty in the morning.' She glanced over at Colin for a moment, still at the mirror, then down at the entries in the motel registration book open on the desk. 'Mr Ware?'

'Yes.'

'Do you have any urgent business this morning?'

'No.'

'Then why don't you go to your room and get a few hours sleep. I'll hold your calls, and you can tell me when you want a wake-up.'

Colin turned around toward her.

'How does that sound.'

'There won't be any calls. I don't know anybody in America.'

'You don't.'

'No.'

'Well maybe a call from someone in England.'

23

'No one there knows where I am.'

She looked at him a moment longer, then picked several wilted flowers from a bouquet in a vase on the desk. 'Two English businessmen stayed here last month,' she said, dropping the flowers into a wastebasket beside the desk. 'They were trying to find stores to carry their software products. But you don't seem to be here on business.'

There was a chair in the corner. 'Can I sit down a moment?'

'Of course.'

'You know,' he said, walking slowly across the room to the chair, 'I've never realised before what it means when people say they're too tired to sleep.' He slumped down into the chair. 'When I filled out the customs form, I put for the purpose of my trip that I was on holiday. I couldn't think of what else to write.'

Joanie studied him a few moments, his eyes fixed on the floor between his shoes.

'Be sure and help yourself to any of our brochures that look interesting.'

'Thank you,' he said without looking up.

It was quiet a few moments.

'Do you like dog racing?'

'Dog racing.'

'Would visiting a greyhound track give you a lift?'

He shook his head, and again it was quiet.

'Mr Ware?' she said finally. 'I don't like to see one of our guests so gloomy.'

'I'm ashamed to be this way.'

'Well you shouldn't be ashamed,' she said. 'I'm just sorry I can't think of something to give you a lasting memory or two to take back to England.'

'The reason I'm here is to try and get rid of a memory I already have.'

'Oh?'

'But I can't,' he said, shutting his eyes tightly.

Once again it was silent.

'Well Mr Ware?'

'Yes?'

'A memory of what.'

'A woman.'

She pursed her lips momentarily.

'A woman,' he repeated. He put his fist up against his forehead.

'An English woman?'

'Half English,' he said, lowering his hand again.

'And half what else.'

'Her father's Welsh. Look, don't pay any attention to this. I'm just utterly . . .'

25

'Well New Cardiff was founded by Welsh people, you know.'

He nodded.

'In 1759 fourteen families migrated here from their small mining community in southern Wales, after having heard there were rich coal deposits in this region. They founded the town, calling it New Cardiff after that city in their homeland, but it soon became evident there were no coal deposits here after all, and they moved on.'

Colin raised his head and looked up at her across the office. 'No deposits,' he said.

'None.'

'Well who told them there were.'

'I don't know that,' she said, brushing some petals off the desk, 'but after they left here they went down to eastern Pennsylvania, a region rich in high-grade coal, where they founded a new community that was soon thriving, and where many other Welsh immigrants soon travelled to join the original settlers, when news of their success spread back to the Old World.'

'That might have been an unconscious reason I got off here,' Colin said. 'The connection between Cardiff and Vera.'

'Her father probably isn't a coal miner,' Joanie said.

'Vera's? No.'

'The man at our Chamber of Commerce always likes us to be on the lookout for promotional tie-ins for the town.'

'He's a bursar at London University.'

'I don't think Doug could use that.'

Colin looked back down at the floor.

'Well I hope that connection doesn't make it harder to forget Vera.'

'It probably will.'

'So you just basically broke up with her then.'

Reaching into his back pocket, Colin got up from the chair. 'This came three days ago,' he said, removing a white card and opening it as he went across the office to her. 'Her wedding invitation.'

Joanie took it from him and held it a few moments as she read it. 'The wedding's on the fourteenth.'

'I know.'

'That's tomorrow.'

'At three P.M.,' Colin said.

'I'm very sorry, Mr Ware.'

'I've never heard of the person she's marrying. I'd never even heard his name before reading it on the invitation.'

'Roger Pelham,' she read.

'I've never heard of Roger Pelham.'

'Well were you and Vera close?' she said, handing back the invitation.

Colin folded it and returned it to his pocket. 'She was my life.'

'Your life.'

'Yes.'

'And what did she say, Mr Ware, when you asked her about the wedding.'

'She wouldn't see me. I was sure it was a joke. Not a very funny one, but that's what I thought. I went over to her flat, thinking we'd sit down at the kitchen table and have a laugh about her rather odd joke.' He looked down at the seat of the chair.

'But she wouldn't talk to you?'

'Her sister was there,' he said, seating himself again. 'It was obvious they were expecting me. She said, "The invitation's Vera's way of telling you your engagement is off."'

'Well that would make the point, wouldn't it.'

'"I want to see her," I said. "I have to see her." "No," Alicia said, "she won't see you, and what's more you're not really invited to the wedding. That was just her way of letting you know where things stand. And if you try and come, the ushers have instructions to stop you. And they've all been given your picture so don't try to get in with a false name."' Colin shook his head again, closing his eyes.

Joanie took a step back so she could glance down for a moment at the open register on the desk. 'Colin?' she said.

'Please, please forgive my talking about this,' he said, 'but I do not feel I'm probably going to get through it.'

'Of course you are,' Joanie said, going over to him. 'Now tell me about her. Just talk to me about Vera for a minute or two.'

'She's just a very beautiful, sensitive person, that's really all I can say about her.'

'She may be beautiful,' Joanie said, 'but she's hardly sensitive, Colin, to do something like that to someone. You say she's your life.'

'More than my life.'

'How long have you known her.'

'Since before we could talk.'

Joanie frowned. 'Well how did you communicate.'

'Our parents were good friends before we were born. The two families were always seeing each other, doing things over the years. Vera and I pretty much grew up together.' He shook his head. 'Was that the problem? That we were like brother and sister? That we were too close?'

The phone rang.

'Excuse me, Colin.' Joanie stepped to the desk to pick it up. 'Battlefield Inn.' She nodded. 'Mandy, I'm with an English guest right now. Let me call you back.'

'I'm interfering with the smooth running of your business,' Colin said, as she hung up.

'It was just Mandy,' she said, returning to him. 'Now.' She put her hand on his shoulder. 'Colin, I want you to talk to me about Vera.'

'What's the point.'

'The point is you're Fisher's and my guest and part of our job is to do everything in our power to see that our guests enjoy themselves. If that means someone has to talk an ex-girlfriend out of his system, so be it.'

'But you're going beyond the requirements of motel management.'

'Were you intimate?' she said. 'You don't have to tell me if you don't want.'

'Intimate.'

'You and Vera.'

'In what respect.'

She shrugged. 'Physically.'

Colin nodded. 'Yes.'

'Do you want to talk at all about that part of it?'

'About intimacy between me and Vera?'

'Often that area can be a source of much of the pain of breaking up.'

'That's true.'

'Very often.'

'But I mean I wouldn't say that was really the basis of our relationship.'

'Not if you knew each other as babies, no.'

Suddenly Colin smiled.

'What,' she said.

He shook his head.

'Really. What were you smiling about.'

'You brought up intimacy,' he said, still shaking his head, 'and sometimes I just can't help smiling when I think about our first time together.'

'Yours and Vera's.'

'But I mean I wouldn't even be talking like this if I wasn't so exhausted I don't even know where I am.'

'Your and Vera's first time.'

'Right,' he said, smiling again.

'And Colin,' she said, 'let me just tell you something here for a moment. No matter what else happens, you will always have that special memory to look back on and treasure.'

Colin looked up at the ceiling and laughed.

'Would it help to talk to me about it.'

'I'm not laughing because it's a happy memory. Just the absurdity of it.'

'Colin, only tell me about it if you feel perfectly comfortable.'

'I'm trying to think how old we were at the time,' he said. 'Seventeen? Maybe sixteen. Could it have been fifteen?'

'Don't worry about that part of it.'

'Anyway, we'd been talking about it for months. Planning it. When shall we do it. Where shall we do it.'

'A couple of nervous teenagers,' Joanie said.

'So we finally did make the decision, which was to do it one Sunday evening over at her grandparents' house.'

'Grandparents,' Joanie laughed.

'Because every Sunday evening, at five o'clock, like clockwork, they went out to eat their big meal of the week.'

'Oh marvellous,' Joanie said. 'Sit down again, Colin.' She helped him back into the chair.

'But the funny part,' Colin said, 'was that they always went to the same restaurant, Sunday after Sunday, week in and week out, and the restaurant they went to – and this is the ridiculous part – was directly across the street from the house they lived in.'

'Oh my God,' Joanie said, clapping her hands together.

'Let me . . .'

'Go on, Colin.'

'Okay,' Colin said, standing up again. 'So over we went, to her nana's house . . .'

'Her nana's house, I love it.'

'We went over there about – I don't know – half past four . . .'

'In the afternoon.'

'Right.'

'Go on.'

'We'd told them the reason we wanted to come over was to watch something on this new large television they'd just got. So we went in, sat down and pretended to be watching some BBC thing on birds in the Orkneys or something.'

'Waiting for them to leave.'

'Right.'

'Which they did exactly at five,' Joanie said.

'Yes.'

'This is beyond priceless.'

'And up the stairs Vera and I went, the minute they were out the door.'

'I think it really is helping you to talk about this,' Joanie said, 'don't you?'

'I'm just so sleep deprived I can't help it."

'You went upstairs.'

'To her grandparents' room,' he said, 'which was in the front of the house. They had a very small house, a terraced house.'

'A what?'

'Terraced house.'

'What's that.'

'What's a terraced house?'

'Oh, oh, oh,' she said. 'A terraced house. Go on. I'm sorry.'

'So there we were. In the front room. Their bedroom. And you know what was directly across the street through the big front window.'

'What.'

'The restaurant.'

'You could see it?'

'It dominated the view.'

'Oh my God,' she said, throwing back her head.

'As I think back about this,' Colin said, reaching up to wipe his eye with the back of his hand, 'I have no idea how we could have been so serious under the circumstances.'

'The first time is always serious, Colin.'

'That's what it was.'

'So there you were, the two of you, up in Nana's bedroom.'

Colin nodded. 'And we just went ahead.'

'You just went ahead with it.'

He shrugged. 'Almost like we'd done it a hundred times before. That's how close we were.'

'On her grandparents' bed.'

'No, not on the bed.'

'Where.'

'You don't want to hear all this.'

'Colin, it's helping you. Don't question.'

'On the chair.'

She nodded. 'Okay.'

'Their easy chair,' he said, 'so we could look out the window.'

'Why would you want to do that.'

'Because one of them could have forgotten something.'

'Oh I see.'

'One of them could have had to come back across the street for something.'

'Seniors can be forgetful.'

'So we just . . . you know . . .'

It was quiet a moment.

'What.'

'What,' Colin repeated.

She made a motion with her hand. 'You were going to say . . .'

'We just . . . proceeded.'

'Colin, you're coming back to life here as we speak.'

'Details of it?'

'You mustn't regress.'

Colin shrugged. 'We took our trousers down.'

'Vera was wearing trousers,' Joanie said.

'As best I can remember. That's what she always wore back then.'

'Levi's?'

'What?'

'Just go on.'

'I don't remember what brand they were, but the next thing we did was to move the chair over next to window so we could keep an eye out.'

'On the restaurant.'

'Yes.'

'And you got in the chair.'

'Sort of on it, really. Sort of draped across it, as I think back. It was a very small chair. You know, I don't really see how we did get into that position.' Again he began to smile. 'But here's the part I don't think you'll believe.'

'I'll believe it, Colin.'

'I hardly do myself.'

'Tell me.'

'The waiter had seated her grandparents – listen to this . . .'

'I'm listening.'

'He'd seated them at the table by the front window.of the restaurant.'

'Oh no.'

'So there Vera and I were, on this tiny chair, having sex for the first time in either of our lives, craning our necks around at the same time and watching her nana and granddad eating shepherd's pie across the street.'

Joanie whooped.

'Without a doubt,' Colin said, again wiping at his eye, 'I would have to say that was the most bizarre situation I've ever been in. Ever. Bar none.'

'I've never heard anything that funny before in my life,' Joanie said, wiping at one of her own eyes.

'Oh Jesus!' Suddenly Colin sat down again, heavily, in the chair. 'Oh Jesus!' He put his face in his hands. 'Oh God!' He began shaking his head.

Joanie hurried to him. 'I want you to do something for me,' she said, taking his elbow. 'First stand up.' She tried to help him up from the chair. 'Colin.'

'Oh God.'

'Here comes another guest.'

He looked up. Through the window he could see an elderly woman approaching the office. 'God help me,' he said, getting to his feet.

'Here we go.'

They walked slowly to the door. As they opened it, the woman was standing just outside. 'This card won't open my door today,' she said, holding a plastic card up in front of Joanie. 'It worked fine yesterday.'

'I need to reprogram it,' Joanie said, helping Colin out past her. 'Can you just wait in the office for a minute and I'll be right back.'

She was frowning at them.

'Just go inside, please.'

The woman stepped inside the office.

'We have some wonderful brochures over there.'

'I saw those yesterday.'

Joanie closed the office door.

'Never before in my life have I acted this way with a stranger,' Colin said.

'Come on, Colin.' Keeping hold of his elbow, she led him along beside the building.

'When you think of British people after this,' he said, stumbling, 'please think of those businessmen who were here last month.'

They stopped beside a large sliding door. 'Wait for me here, Colin.'

'I'm not representative.'

She slid open the door and went inside.

On the other side of the driveway was the motel swimming pool, and floating on the surface of the pool was one bright red leaf and one yellow one. Bent forward slightly, Colin stared at the two leaves till Joanie returned.

'This'll help you sleep,' she said, stepping through the door, showing him a little white pill. She had a glass of water in her other hand.

'I don't use prescription medication.'

'You do now,' she said, giving it to him. 'And while you're asleep I'm going to call someone, a very good person, a very good friend – Mandy, the one who phoned earlier – and she'll be here when you wake up.'

'I can't see anyone like this.'

'Mandy's a trained care-giver, Colin.'

'A trained what?'

'Care-giver.'

'No,' he said, shaking his head.

'Put this in your mouth,' she said, taking the pill back out of his hand. 'Open.'

'Let me meet your friend in a few days, after I've . . .'

She pushed the pill into his mouth.

'. . . got hold of myself.'

She raised the glass to his lips. 'Swallow.'

'Mrs Fisher.'

'Please call me Joanie.'

'Joanie.'

'Now Mandy's a slightly younger person,' she said, putting one of her hands on the back of his head as she tipped the glass up against his lips, 'but she's one of my very closest friends, and she's just wonderful with people. Swallow, Colin.'

Water ran down over his chin and on to his shirt as he swallowed.

'Did it go down?'

He shook his head.

'Swallow again.'

'Don't tip it so much.'

'Mandy has two weeks off,' Joanie said, as he took another swallow. 'She's just starting her second week so this works out perfectly.'

'Two weeks off from what.'

'Did it go down?'

'Yes.'

Joanie poured the rest of the water into a potted plant beside them. 'Shining Shores,' she said.

'What's that.'

'It's our nursing home.'

'She works at a nursing home?'

'And she's getting very depressed during her break, with nothing to do. She's begun calling me two and three times a day, not that I would ever begrudge Mandy the time . . .' She turned Colin, pointing him toward his room. '. . . but after all, I do have a motel to run during the height of Foliage Season.' She helped him start moving forward. 'So for her to have a care-giving challenge like this just show up on her doorstep almost seems like a gift from above.' She let go of him. 'Can you make it the rest of the way?'

'I can,' he said, walking forward on his own.

'Are you sure?'

'Yes.'

'You're in good hands here, Colin,' she said after him.

'I know,' Colin said. 'Thank you. Goodbye.'

3

There was a damp, warm sensation on Colin's forehead when he woke up. It moved slowly down one side of his face, then up the other. He opened his eyes. A young woman was seated in the chair beside his bed, holding her finger over her lips. 'Shhh,' she said. With her other hand she moved the moist washcloth over his face again.

'Mandy,' Colin said.

She placed her fingers over his eyes and closed them.

'You are Mandy,' he said with them shut.

'Don't worry about who I am,' she said quietly. 'But I just want you to do one thing for me.'

'What's that.'

'You don't have to talk,' she said, 'but I want you to think of the most peaceful place you've ever been. Just nod if you're willing to do that for me.'

Colin nodded.

'Try and think of a place so peaceful that one day you'd like to go back there and stay a long, long time. Will you do that for me?'

'If you'd like.'

'Don't talk. Just nod.'

He nodded.

'And if you can,' she said, 'try and make this place you're thinking of a place that's beyond time and space itself.' She set down her washcloth and began to massage his forehead. 'Are you doing that?'

He shook his head.

'You're not?'

Again he shook it.

'Why aren't you doing that. You can talk to tell me.'

'Beyond time and space,' he said. 'What does that mean.'

'What does it mean?'

'I have no concept of it.'

'Well it's kind of hard to explain,' she said after a moment. 'Look, just think of a peaceful place.' She moved her hand down from his forehead and over his eyes for a moment, then went back to massaging him.

'Are you doing it?'

'Yes.'

'You're thinking of the most peaceful place you've ever been.'

'One of them.'

'And do you want to tell me what it is?'

'A beach.'

She pressed her thumbs in against his temples. 'And where is this peaceful beach.'

'The Canaries.'

'Where?'

'The Canary Islands.'

'Where's that.'

'Off the coast of Spain.'

'And what were you doing there.'

'Vera's best friend at the time worked for Thomas Cook,' he said. 'We got a special fare.'

'Vera.'

'Yes.'

'The person you came here to forget?'

'Yes.'

'Okay, well you shouldn't make it a place you went with her.' She began massaging Colin's scalp. 'Think of the most peaceful place you've ever been without her.'

He was quiet as she continued to go over the top of his head with her fingers. 'Okay.'

'Do you have it?'

'Yes.'

'And do you want to tell me what it is.'

'A forest.'

She nodded. 'In England?'

'Could I just say something a little off the subject.'

'Just tell me if the forest is in England.'

'It is.'

'And do you feel perfectly peaceful there?'

'Yes, but I'm—'

'And is it a beautiful, quiet, restful place you wish you could stay in for ever and ever?'

Colin opened his eyes. 'Not to change the subject,' he said, 'but is this a care-giving technique of some sort you're doing?'

'I guess you could call it that.'

'That you learned where you work.'

'I learned it in training. I apply it where I work.'

'Right,' he said, 'but my point is, I don't think I'm exactly the type of person it's meant to be applied to.'

'Don't you like to feel peaceful?'

'I like to feel peaceful,' he said, raising himself up on his elbow. 'I'm just saying I think the terminology you're using is tailored for someone in a slightly different situation.'

'It's tailored for people who are preparing for their Journey,' she said.

'Their Journey.'

'That's what we call it.'

'I see. And do I strike you as someone who's preparing for my Journey?'

'You might be. From what Joanie said.'

'And what did Joanie say.'

'Well that's sort of confidential.'

Colin raised up on both elbows. 'Why.'

'You just always treat that type of information confidentially.'

'Where you work you treat it confidentially.'

'That's right.'

'But this is a motel.'

'I'm aware of that.'

'Well listen.' He sat the rest of the way up. 'You really have helped, but I think this is probably as relaxed as I'm going to get for now.'

'Could I ask you something?' she said.

'Of course.'

'You're here to forget this person Vera,' she said.

'And get away from the things I associate with her.'

'But here's what I don't get,' Mandy said, 'and I'm not trying to be rude.'

'No.'

'I mean why New Cardiff,' she said. 'Do you know anyone here?'

'No.'

'Have you ever been here before.'

'I haven't.'

'Well did you hear about the town or something when you were over in England?'

'No.'

She shrugged. 'Like I say, I'm sorry to be rude, but what are you doing here. I know I shouldn't be so curious, but I just am.'

'A person has every right to know why someone's in their town.'

'I mean when you got on the bus, why did you buy your ticket for here?'

'I didn't. I bought it for somewhere in Maine.'

'Well so why did you get off here.'

'I noticed the monument.'

When she didn't respond for a few moments, he turned toward her. She was looking down at the carpet.

'The Battlefield Monument,' he said.

She remained quiet for several more seconds.

'Mandy?'

'Yes.'

'Are you all right?'

'You just saw it out the window?' she said, looking back at him.

'There it was.'

'And that's the only reason you got off.'

'This seems hard for people to grasp,' Colin said, frowning for a moment. 'Let me think if there were any others.'

Mandy was sitting very still in the chair.

'Someone tried to flush an apple down the toilet in Connecticut,' he said, 'so that was broken. I suppose that was a minor consideration.'

'Look, the monument was a good reason.'

'It doesn't show a very comprehensive attitude toward travel planning, does it.'

Suddenly Mandy got to her feet. She took a deep breath. 'Shall we go over there?'

'The monument?'

'I'll be happy to take you,' she said, pointing toward the door. 'My car's right outside.'

'Now?'

'If you want to.'

'Well I'm sort of waiting for Fisher right now.'

'It's extremely interesting,' she said. 'Do you know how it's set up?'

'No, I . . .'

'Okay,' she said, 'well down at the bottom they have this display case with little soldiers fighting in it – that's very realistic. Then you go up the elevator and they have a recording at the top telling the different things you can see out on the landscape. Like this hill where the Redcoats had a cannon and everybody came charging up to try and get it away from them. That's really fascinating.'

'It sounds very well put together,' he said after a few moments.

'Oh it is,' she said. 'How about tomorrow.'

He looked at her as she waited for him to answer. 'Is there some great rush about my seeing it?'

'Of course not.'

'It's not going anywhere, is it.'

'No, it's just that I'm off this week, and it would be convenient to show it to you.' Again it was quiet as she waited.

'What time does it open.'

'At least by ten,' she said. 'I can find out.'

'Do you want to pick me up at ten-thirty?'

'Yes I do,' she said, going to the door. 'I'll be in front.'

After she had gone Colin rested back on his elbows again and remained there several minutes longer, looking across the room at a little peep-hole at eye-level in the door. He listened as a car drove up in front of the room next to his, then as someone got out and went into the room, then a minute or two later as the muffled sound of a television reached him through the wall.

Finally he got up and walked into the bathroom. On the wall above the toilet was a frame, and in the frame, in letters printed to look like red and green yarn stitched on cloth, were the words 'Our Very Favorite Guest Is Reading This Sign'. Colin looked at it a few more moments, then went to the sink and opened his shaving case.

4

It wasn't till almost evening that Fisher returned from delivering the table to his son, but he was enthusiastic about sitting for his portrait and wanted to put everything else aside while Colin did the drawing. 'Whenever Brad and I get together we wind up eating a ton of burgers between us,' he said after they'd gone into the Fisher living room, where it had been decided the portrait would be done, 'so Joanie can go ahead with her dinner now and I'll grab something later. How about you.'

Colin had gone to turn on a floor lamp standing in the corner of the room.

'How about you, Colin. Dinnerwise.'

'I had a sandwich across the street.'

'No way that's going to hold you till morning.'

Colin turned the lamp off again and went to the wall where there was another one, on the end of a wooden bar that could be swung out into the room. 'Why don't we try something a little different with our lighting,' he said, bringing the lamp out from the wall. 'Can you sit there?' He nodded at a chair.

Fisher seated himself.

'I might try bringing this right above.' He moved the lamp over the top of Fisher's head. 'How do you turn it on.'

Fisher twisted around and reached up to turn it on for him. 'You're going to light me from the top?'

'I'm thinking of it.' He stepped back to study Fisher's face in the light. 'Scoot the chair back about five inches.'

Remaining seated, Fisher pushed the chair back across the carpet till Colin raised his hand for him to stop.

'You have a naturally dramatic face,' Colin said. 'If this works out we'll be able to emphasise that quality even more.'

'Dramatic,' Fisher said.

Colin put his finger on Fisher's chin and pushed his face slightly to the left. 'Just try to hold it there.' With his other hand he reached up to pull the lamp down closer to the top of Fisher's head. 'Is that a position you can maintain for thirty minutes or so?'

'I can do it.'

'Put your hands comfortably in your lap.'

Fisher rested them there. Colin went to a sofa against the wall, seated himself and picked up his sketch pad from the coffee table where he'd set it before.

'About the last thing in my mind when I went out of here this morning was that I'd be sitting for my portrait when I came back.'

'Thank you for agreeing on such short notice.'

'Are we allowed to talk?' Fisher said.

'We can talk calmly.'

'Because I was going to ask you – you're a professional artist over there in London?'

Colin picked up one of the pencils he'd set in a row on the table. 'Something about that word always rubs me slightly the wrong way,' he said, looking back up at Fisher, 'but I guess that's what I am.'

'"Professional" rubs you the wrong way?'

'May I ask you to tip your head back up again the way it was.'

Fisher tipped his head up.

'Maybe not quite that much.'

He tipped it down again.

'Sometimes it helps to hold the head still by keeping our eyes on a fixed point.' Colin opened his pad to the first page, then sat quietly studying Fisher's face.

'Joanie told me what happened over there in your homeland.'

Colin raised his arm and held his pencil out toward Fisher.

'Getting the rug pulled out from under you like that would be nobody's idea of fun.'

Colin closed one eye and moved the pencil back and forth slowly as he looked at Fisher's chin.

'But listen, my friend,' Fisher said, 'once the pain wears off you'll be a far better and stronger man than if it never happened at all.'

'If it ever does,' Colin said quietly.

'Excuse me?'

'I said, "If it ever does wear off."'

'Oh it will. One thing about pain – it will wear off.'

Colin lowered the pencil, and after making several large circles above the paper with his hand, looking back and forth between Fisher and the pad as he did, he drew the outline of Fisher's head. 'Actually I may have made a start in figuring out what happened there,' he said. 'As I was shaving this afternoon a possible explanation for her behaviour did occur to me. The head's sinking.'

Fisher raised his head.

Colin looked down at the circle he'd made, then lightly sketched in one of Fisher's eyes.

'What explanation is that,' Fisher said, 'if it's not too personal.'

'When I first thought of it, it seemed bizarre, but this whole experience is so bizarre I really don't feel I can rule anything out.'

'What was it.'

'About a year ago,' Colin said, carefully drawing the other eye, 'maybe a little more than that, Vera started taking some yoga lessons. She'd been talking about taking them for years, and she finally just went ahead and joined a little yoga school. Your head's nice and steady now.'

'I'm focusing on the plant over there by the door,' he said. 'So she signed up at the yoga school.'

'It was over in the Strand.'

'Okay.'

'And it made her happy, she obviously enjoyed it, but I think it was because she was enjoying it that I didn't notice at first she didn't particularly like talking about the sessions – they were twice a week, then increased to three times weekly.' He brushed at the page with his fingers. 'She mentioned that – how often she went – but really that was about all she had to say on the subject. And maybe that was the first clue.'

'What's that.'

'It was something we weren't talking about the way we talked about everything else.'

Fisher nodded.

'Careful.'

He stopped nodding.

'But of course the major clue was probably Swami himself, and the way she talked about him when she did say anything.'

'Who?'

'Swami.'

'Oh I see.'

'For example,' Colin said, darkening Fisher's eye, 'we'd be sitting in a restaurant somewhere, when suddenly she'd put her fork down and say, "Oh I don't think Swami would want me to be eating this."' He began pencilling in the other eye. 'Or just walking down the street together, looking in shop windows, and it would be, "Oh my God, it's after five – Swami's going to kill me if I don't do my afternoon cobra."'

'Her what?'

'It's an exercise.'

'Oh.'

'But my point is, there were these hints. In retrospect. To which I was wholly oblivious at the time.'

'You don't think she ran off with Swami.'

'Oh no. But I do think that's where she may have met this Roger Pelham.' Colin returned his pencil to the table and chose another. 'A while into the course they started these exercises with partners. And I remember she hated those at first. He'd have them sit down on the floor, back-to-back, and lock arms – this is the one exercise she did tell me about in detail. Then they'd pull against each other and chant.'

'Oh boy.'

Colin streaked in Fisher's hair with the new pencil. 'At first she really objected to that. She was talking about quitting the pro-gramme just because of the partner exercises.' Again he brushed at the page. 'And now as I think back,' he said, 'those complaints about the partner thing may have been her first cry for help. Which went unheard.' He took another pencil and looked up at Fisher's nose. 'Because they stopped.'

'What did.'

'Her complaints,' he said, 'and I'm wondering if it wasn't at that point that I lost her.'

'When her complaints stopped.'

'When her cries for help, if that's what they were, to which there was no response from me, stopped. Yes.'

Colin looked over to see Joanie standing in the doorway. 'Would you like a cup of tea or anything, Colin?'

'I'm fine, thank you.'

'Fisher?'

'I can't turn my head right now, Joanie. I'll talk to you later.'

She stood a few moments watching as Colin went back to drawing her husband. 'Should that dark shadow be coming down over Fisher's mouth like that?'

'It should,' Fisher said.

'Fisher has such nice lips,' she said. 'I hope they'll show.'

'They'll be shown to full advantage,' Colin said.

'Fisher's lips are so—'

'Let the man work, Joanie.'

She went back into the other room, and it was quiet for a while as Colin sketched.

'Colin?' Fisher said finally.

'Yes.'

'Could we be talking cult here, by any chance?'

Colin placed his thumb lightly on the drawing and rubbed it slowly back and forth a few times over Fisher's hair.

'From what you've said – Swamis and whatnot, breakdown of communication – I'm thinking we may be talking cult here.'

Colin continued to blend Fisher's hair with his thumb. 'At first I used to pick her up from her sessions – just to have an excuse, really, to see each other. She could have got back by herself, but we just liked being together.'

'Sure.'

'But then, after a while, she seemed not to want me to keep meeting her – "Oh it's too much trouble for you," that sort of thing. But as I think back – and I know our minds tend to play tricks on us as we try to explain things that make no sense – but as I was reconstructing all this this afternoon, and I'd remember when I used to sit there waiting for her to come out of the school – and I can't allow my imagination to run away with me – but I swear, looking out the car window at the people going in and out of that building, they all had this sort of fixed look in their eyes, this sort of glazed-over look on all of their faces – I don't think I'm making that up.'

Fisher began nodding. 'My friend, I hate to say this, because I know how much you love her, but the fact is you've lost your good woman to a cult.'

'The head.'

'Sorry.' He held still. 'Now the first thing you're going to go through on this thing is the denial stage. In fact that's where you are now. And it's a perfectly healthy reaction, Colin. Is she a wealthy individual?'

'Vera? Oh no.'

'Because these cults will target a person with money.'

'I mean she does well enough. She has a little stall.'

'A what?'

'A stall. In Covent Garden.'

'A store is this?'

'Vera's Treasures, she calls it.'

'What sort of merchandise.'

'This and that,' Colin said. 'An imported handbag or two. Earrings. The odd necklace.' He picked up a pencil. 'But Vera in a cult?' He shook his head.

'Colin, as it happens I've done a bit of reading on this very subject. And let me tell you, some of the stuff that's going on out there makes your hair stand on end.'

He began shading the area under Fisher's nose. 'Vera's too intelligent for something like that.'

'One of the books was by a physics professor who was a former cult member. Intelligence has nothing to do with it.'

Colin stopped drawing. 'Could Swami have put her together with the partner, and she was fighting it at first, then when I was oblivious to her signal for help she succumbed? And could the partner she was rocking back and forth with all that time have been Roger Pelham?'

'Don't blame yourself, Colin – that's very important.'

'But is that the explanation for all this?'

'Yes, Colin. And tough as it is, it's best for you to face it now.'

Colin's head fell forward and for several moments it was perfectly quiet in the room.

'We have a saying here in America,' Fisher said finally, not moving his face. 'It goes "Don't throw good money after bad". And that's the way you need to look at the situation with this Vera.'

'Actually I may have heard that saying in my own country.'

'Well it originated here,' Fisher said, 'and every time you start to get depressed I want you to say it to yourself.'

'I'm not sure I see exactly how it fits.'

'Just keep saying it. You will.'

'But I'm not even sure that's what happened. How do I know the yoga explanation isn't just some pathetic lie I'm telling myself so I don't have to admit she simply fell out of love with me.'

'No.'

'It's not?'

'The people with the glazed expressions going in and out of the school,' Fisher said. 'My heart sank for you when you told me that, but at least I knew you'd put two and two together.'

Colin stared down at the partially completed drawing in his lap.

'And all you have any business thinking about at this point, Colin, is moving on.'

'Moving on,' Colin said softly after a few more seconds had passed, his head still bowed.

'Getting those eyes of yours back on the prize again.'

Colin nodded. 'Yes.'

'And you've come to the right place to do it.'

'The motel?'

'No, America.'

'Oh. Yes.'

'I think you'll find we don't spend a lot of time worrying about water under the bridge here.'

Colin looked at his row of pencils on the table. 'No.'

'So learn that little trick from us.'

'I want to.'

'Where you come from maybe folks like to sit around chewing on the past,' Fisher said, raising his head slightly, 'but over here that ain't done much.'

Colin took his next pencil. 'Ain't done much,' he repeated.

'No time for that.'

Colin waited a few moments, then looked back at his subject. 'Thank you. I needed you to say that to me, Fisher. Thank you for those valuable words.'

5

Mandy was very quiet the next morning on the drive between the motel and the monument.

'I doubt that most motel operators would take the personal interest in their guests that Fisher and your friend Joanie have shown me,' Colin said, as they turned out the entrance and on to the highway. 'Are they that attentive to everyone who stays here?'

'I couldn't really say.' She kept her hands on the steering wheel and her eyes forward, but said nothing more.

A few minutes later, as the tall grey obelisk was looming over the tops of the trees ahead of them, Colin said, 'I took a little walk around New Cardiff this morning, and I must have counted three shopping centres in less than a mile. I couldn't help wondering how a small town like this supports all that business.'

But again Mandy's face remained forward, her only response being a shrug.

Several cars were parked at the kerb that surrounded the large grassy circle from which the monument rose. Mandy drove past a bus with the words Heritage Tours on its side, then turned in toward the kerb and went forward till she'd gone halfway around the circle and no other vehicles were nearby. 'Before we get out,' she said, turning off the engine, 'could I say something?'

'Of course.'

'Something I feel so badly about I didn't sleep last night.'

'I know the feeling,' Colin said.

'To feel that badly?' she said, turning to look at him.

'To be that tired.'

'I don't mind being tired,' she said, 'but I didn't even figure out the thing I lay awake all night worrying about. You'd think at least I'd have gotten that out of it.'

'What was it,' Colin said. 'Or should I ask.'

Mandy reached across him to open the door of the glove compartment, and took out a small bottle. 'Peach brandy,' she said, showing Colin the label. 'I don't suppose you want any.'

'Not this morning.'

'This is what I felt so badly about all night.' She twisted the cap of the bottle and there was a crackling noise as the seal broke.

'Peach brandy.'

'It's something I have to do,' she said. 'I have to go back into the past.' She turned to look at him again.

'Right now?'

'Yes.'

Colin nodded.

'But that's what I lay awake about,' she said. 'I have to apologise to you for this, but once I start doing it I'm afraid it won't seem like my apology was very sincere.'

'Apologise for what,' he said.

'Inviting you to see the monument and then getting drunk.'

Colin shrugged. 'You're on holiday,' he said. 'It's not up to me to criticise you.'

'But I was telling you all that stuff about cannons and soldiers charging up hills to get you here. Then I do this.'

'Maybe you're afraid of heights,' he said. 'Some people need a few drinks before flying. Maybe you need to steady yourself before going to the top of the monument.'

'It's not that.' She unscrewed the lid from the bottle, but then sat quietly holding it.

'Look,' Colin said at last, 'you don't owe me an apology. I'll enjoy myself in any case.'

'At least this shouldn't take long,' she said, putting the bottle to her lips. 'I haven't been drunk for years.'

He watched her take several gulps.

'You'll probably have to drive us back though,' she said.

'I will?'

'After we visit the monument.'

'Well that may not work out,' Colin said.

'You don't drive?'

'Not on the right-hand side.'

'Oh, I forgot.' She looked down at her bottle for a few moments. 'Well look, I can keep my eyes out and let you know if you're starting to veer over to the other side. But if it's me driving we'll be on the wrong side of the road the whole way.' She took another swallow.

'You said this had something to do with your past?'

She nodded. 'My past,' she said. 'And you.'

Colin's attention was caught by a man who had come to stand on the grass several yards away from their car and who was aiming his camera up at the top of the monument.

'Me and your past.'

'That's right.'

'How do I fit into your past.'

'You just do.'

'A past life?'

'Oh no. I don't believe in anything like that.'

'Because it's not like we go back.'

'No.'

'If we wanted to sit around reminiscing,' he said, 'we shouldn't really bother to sit down.'

The man on the grass snapped a picture of the towering obelisk as Mandy took another swallow of the brandy. 'Colin?' she said, lowering the bottle. 'You know yesterday when Joanie was telling you about me?'

He nodded.

'Did Joanie tell you I'm depressed because I don't have the job to keep me busy at the moment?'

'She said she hoped I would provide a care-giving challenge to lift your spirits.'

'Because that's not what I need,' she said.

'It's not.'

'No. I need more than that.'

On the other side of the windscreen the man was motioning for his wife to stand in front of the monument.

'What more do you need.'

She held up the bottle to see how much was left. 'I don't think I can put it into words.'

'Try.'

'I mean I really feel like I'm helping people over at the Shores. And I've never had that feeling before. Which is really good.'

The man clicked his wife's picture, then she walked to him, took the camera and waited as he went to stand where she had been before.

'God! You came here for a historical reason. How can I be doing this. How can I be getting drunk when you just want to experience the historical atmosphere.'

'I'm experiencing it.'

'How could you be. With some crazy getting wasted beside you in her car.'

'It's seeping through.'

Suddenly the man whose wife was preparing to take his picture fell down on the grass as he walked backwards to get closer to the monument.

'Oh Jesus.' Mandy came forward in her seat.

'He's okay,' Colin said.

His wife laughed as the man got to his feet.

'He just tripped.'

'I thought he had a heart attack.' Mandy sat back. 'That's what I'm like now. I always think everyone's going to die. Someone will cough behind me in line in the supermarket and I'll expect them to fall over dead. The other day I turned around and said, "Are you all right?" in this real serious way to some woman who

72

had just cleared her throat and she thought I was a total nut-case.'

'It's hard to leave your work behind at the end of the day,' Colin said.

'It gets harder and harder.'

The woman finished snapping her husband's photograph and they walked away. Mandy looked at the bottle in her hand. 'If you put all of this stuff I drank during high school in one place,' she said, 'it would fill up a lake. People I see from those days still call me Brandy Mandy.'

He watched her take another swallow.

'God, what we used to do up there.' She leaned forward so she could look up through the windscreen to the top of the monument.

'Non-historical things?'

She laughed, then covered her mouth to stop herself. 'What didn't we used to do up there is more like it.' She burst out laughing, but then stopped suddenly again, again covering her mouth.

'You know something,' Colin said, watching a group of older tourists coming out of the monument's entrance, 'I wonder whether this is really the best time to take this in.' Up at the top he could see the heads of several visitors looking out through an opening in the stone.

'Oh Jesus, I just remembered what Randy Carr and Kathy Lewis and Frankie Overmaster and me did up there one afternoon.' She tried to stifle another laugh.

'Mandy.'

'I'd forgotten that time,' she said, looking over at him. 'I'd forgotten what Frankie Overmaster did to me up at the top.' She held up her hand. 'Don't worry, I'm not going to tell you.'

'That's probably best.'

'I'd never tell anybody that.'

'Look, here's my suggestion,' he said, reaching for the bottle.

'There's just a little left.' She raised it to her lips.

'We need to start planning our return to the motel,' Colin said.

'We haven't gone up yet.'

'The historical moment has passed, Mandy.'

'You know something?' she said, holding up the empty bottle. 'If I was back in high school I'd just heave this thing out the window on to the street. Somebody running over broken glass? You think I would have cared about that back then?'

He reached for the bottle.

'Oh I wouldn't throw it out there now,' she said, moving it away from him. 'I'm just making the point of what an incredibly irresponsible person I used to be. And how I've changed.' She tossed the bottle over on to the back seat. 'But in a way I'm not happy to be responsible.'

'Listen, Mandy,' he said, reaching back for it and setting it down on the floor, 'if I drive slowly enough, we may have a fifty-fifty chance of getting back to the motel without becoming statistics.'

'But the monument.'

'It'll be here.'

'I used to get drunk really fast – I just remembered that – but then I'd sober up again just as fast. It must be metabolic.'

Colin rested his hand on the handle of the door beside himself. 'Let me collect my thoughts here a minute.'

'Everyone else would still be staggering around, yelling and pissing on trees, and I'd be sober as a judge again. Maybe that's why I drank so much of it.'

'Here's what I think we should do,' Colin said.

'I loved my high school years. I don't remember them, but I loved them.'

Colin opened the door. 'I'll get in the driving side, and you slide over here.'

'My brother's in high school now. God – can you imagine having a brother ten years younger than you? He was unplanned.'

'Mandy.'

'I told him about you, by the way – I hope that was all right.'

'Told him what.'

'That you're an artist from England,' she said. 'For some unknown reason Rob seems to think he's good looking. So now he wants me to find out if you'll draw his picture.'

'Why does everyone over here feel they have to be good looking for me to draw them?'

Mandy sat back in her seat. 'Two years ago,' she said, 'Rob went born again on us. It's really sad. Wasting your high-school experience as a born-again Christian. "Rob," I tell him, "you're only young once. You have your whole life stretching out ahead of you to be a Christian."'

'I'll get out,' Colin said, 'and you slide over.'

'Right.'

He put his leg out of the car.

'Joanie's great, isn't she?'

'Joanie. Yes.'

'God what a good friend she turned out to be.'

'Here I go out.' He moved farther out of the car.

'But you know something? As great a friend as she is – and she's the best one I have in the world . . .'

Colin reached back in and removed the keys from the ignition switch, then got all the way out of the car.

'As wonderful a friend as Joanie is,' Mandy said, looking out the open door at him, 'she still can't see all the way to the bottom of my heart.'

'Just move carefully over the little gearshift there and to this side.'

'But you know why that is, don't you, Colin.'

'Why what is.'

'Why Joanie can't see all the way into my heart.'

'Actually I don't.'

'It's because two women's friendship with each other can only go so far. But hey, that's nothing against Joanie. It's not her fault.'

'This way, Mandy.'

'Let's face it. Fisher can see places in Joanie's heart that I never will.'

'I'm coming over there, Mandy, I'll help you from your side.' He closed his door and started around the car but by the time he reached the front she had opened her door and was climbing out.

'Go back in, Mandy.'

She came all the way out, turned around and with her back to the car pushed the door shut with her foot. 'Have you ever heard the song called "A Woman's Heart"?'

'Okay, come around to this side then.'

'Have you?'

'"Woman's Heart". No.'

'God it's beautiful,' she said, as he took her arm and helped her around the back of the car. 'Let me think how it goes.'

'Step up over the verge.'

'Now I remember.'

'Up here.'

'"My heart is low",' she sang, stepping up on to the grass. '"My heart is so low. As only a woman's heart can be".'

Keeping hold of her arm, Colin opened the door on his side of the car again.

'Whenever I play that for them at the Shores, everyone just weeps.'

'Here we go.' He moved her toward the door.

'We didn't see it yet,' she said, pointing at the monument.

'Another time, Mandy.'

'No,' she said. 'It has to be now.'

'Mandy.'

'Please. Really. I'm sober.'

'We'll come back tomorrow.'

'You don't understand.'

'Mandy.'

'Please listen to what I'm trying to say,' she said. 'Please.'

'Well I am listening to you, Mandy.'

'You are?'

'Of course.'

'And I can say this?'

'I want you to.'

She took in a deep breath, and then let it out again. 'Yesterday,' she said. 'When you came here yesterday. Or I don't know what day you came, but when I saw you yesterday. When I came over to the motel – Joanie told me about you on the phone and I came over there and she gave me a key to go in your room and I went in there and I saw you sleeping on your bed.' She took another deep breath. 'I'm out of breath for some reason.'

'Mandy.'

'You said you'd let me say this.'

'Go on.'

'I saw you sleeping there. And you were from England. I just knew it was my last chance.'

For a long time it was quiet as she stood looking at him. She stepped back slightly, then forward again.

'Last chance,' Colin said finally.

'Yes.'

'For what.'

She turned her face up toward the monument.

'Last chance for what,' he said again.

'I can't even say it,' she said. 'I got drunk so I could say it, and I still can't.'

'Just blurt it out.'

'I want someone to kiss me up there one last time.'

Colin kept holding her arm as Mandy's eyes remained on the openings at the top of the grey stone obelisk. 'If I asked anyone I know to do it,' she said, 'I'd be the laughing stock of the town. But if I could just go up there one last time and have someone kiss me,

79

then I could quit thinking about how my life's over, how it used to be so much better, which I know isn't even true, but that's all I ever think about any more when I'm working over at Shining Shores, how I wish I was back in high school again. I don't even know what's wrong with me, but I don't want to go on feeling this way the rest of my life, and when I saw you sleeping there I just thought maybe this is the last chance I'll ever have, and then when you said the monument was the whole reason you got off the bus in New Cardiff, I just felt sure it had to be fate or something.' She stepped backwards, pulling her arm out of his grip. ' Oh God, I didn't think this would sound so fucking dumb.'

She pushed some hair away from her face. Then they stood quietly several feet from each other, Mandy looking down at the grass as Colin looked at her.

'I don't know if I could compete with Frankie Overmaster.'

'You don't even have to kiss me on the mouth if you don't want. Just on the cheek would be all right.'

At an observation slit at the top of the monument someone was standing behind one of the mounted telescopes, moving it slowly back and forth to scan the landscape.

Colin held out his hand.

Mandy had forgotten there was road construction closing one of the streets between the monument and the motel, so as they approached the barrier she had to tell Colin to go all the way back to the monument and start over. He pulled to the side of the road and stopped.

'What are you doing.'

'Just resting a moment.'

'Resting.'

'Please, Mandy.' He raised his hand for a second, then took a deep breath.

Mandy shrugged. 'You can go left up ahead, or make a U-turn and go back the way we came.'

'Which has the least traffic.'

'Turning left, but that's the longest.'

Because he had almost hit a dog, and two cars had come up behind him and flashed their headlights into his rear-view mirror, Colin waited beside the road nearly a full minute till no other cars were in sight before driving up to the intersection and making a wide left-hand arc into the other street.

'I have the same initials as Marilyn Monroe,' Mandy said.

He pulled up his leg as a car suddenly sped across the highway in front of them.

'Just keep going straight now,' she said.

He leaned forward as he drove, keeping both hands on the steering wheel. 'Try and tell me a little sooner next time we have to turn.'

'You're doing fine.'

'Why don't you poll some of the other drivers on that subject.'

'I just hope we get back to the motel by this time next year.' She reached over with her leg, pressing down on top of his foot with hers.

'Don't,' he said, as the car lurched forward. 'Seriously.'

Mandy draped her arm out the car window, looking at the passing trees and houses as they drove along. 'Do the trees change colour in England?'

'Not like this.'

'What's the difference over there.'

'Not as many trees. Not as spectacular.'

'It is spectacular,' she said. 'You kind of forget that when you live here and see it year after year.'

Colin veered to the left to correct for driving too close to a car parked at the side of the road.

'What happened.'

'I was drifting,' he said. 'You'd think the problem would be wanting to go into the opposite lane, but it isn't. It's overcompensating and drifting over to the right.'

'Colin?'

'What.'

'What were you thinking about up there.'

He slowed for a stop sign, waited for a car to pass in front of them, then slowly drove forward again. 'What was I thinking about up in the monument?'

'While we were kissing.'

He shrugged. 'I don't know if I was exactly thinking of anything, at least that I can remember.'

'Did you notice that little girl up there?'

'Which.'

'A little red-haired girl. She kept coming over to watch us. And then her mother would pull her away and tell her to look back out at the battlefield.'

'I did notice her.'

'I don't think she'd ever seen two people kissing before.'

'Or that her mother had.'

Mandy pointed ahead. 'Turn right up ahead.'

'By the petrol station?'

'No, the gas station.'

Colin put on his blinker and slowed.

'And you shouldn't get so close to the kerb this time. You went up over it on your last right turn.'

He turned carefully right around the corner without going up across the kerbing.

'Colin?'

'Yes, Mandy.'

'Can I tell you what I was thinking up there in the monument?'

'I'd like you to.'

She looked down at the dashboard. 'I was thinking how if there had never been a Revolutionary War, then there would never have been a Battle of New Cardiff. And if there had never been a

Battle of New Cardiff, they never would have put up the monument. And if they hadn't put up a monument, you wouldn't have seen it out of the bus. And if you hadn't seen it out of the bus, you wouldn't have gotten out here. And if you hadn't gotten out here, we wouldn't have met. And if we hadn't met we wouldn't have been up in the monument.' She looked over at him. 'That's what I was thinking about as we were kissing.'

'It sounds like your mind was racing.'

'It wasn't racing exactly. I was just thinking of all the things that had to have happened for us to be up there.'

Keeping his eyes on the road, he nodded.

'Were you thinking of anything like that?'

'Not consciously.'

'But you might have been thinking of it unconsciously.'

'Unconsciously, anything's possible.'

'I usually don't think about history,' she said, leaning back in her seat, 'but I guess you think about it when you're caught up in it.'

'Caught up in it.'

She nodded.

'You felt you were caught up in history?'

'You didn't, I guess.'

'It didn't occur to me,' he said. 'Maybe I just wasn't aware of it.'

'I was probably just imagining it.'

'But what do you mean.'

'I don't know. I was just thinking about how kissing an English person up in the Revolutionary War Monument was kind of like being caught up in history.' She looked out at a billboard beside the road. 'But I can see that was really stupid.'

There were no cars in front or behind him as Colin drove for a while in silence. 'It wasn't stupid,' he said finally.

'Yes it was.'

'It wasn't,' he said. 'You're just saying if this was still a colony we wouldn't have had anywhere to go and kiss.'

She turned to look at him. 'You're just making fun of me now.'

'No I'm not.'

'Yes you are.'

He took his eyes off the road long enough to glance over at her.

'You know you are.'

'I'll tell you one thing though.'

'What.'

'Of all the colonists I know,' he said, 'none kiss like that.'

She laughed and looked out ahead of them again.

Suddenly a pick-up truck came up behind them and began flashing its headlights and honking. Mandy looked back through the rear window. 'What an asshole,' she said. 'Don't pay any attention.'

There was a squeal of tyres as the vehicle lurched out around them, its driver, in a plaid shirt and black beard, leaning over toward his open window to yell something as he passed.

'Give him the finger,' Mandy said.

'I may not.'

'Did you hear what he just called you?'

'I did,' Colin said, looking at the back of the man's head between the bars of a gun rack as he sped away. 'I'm treating it as a compliment.'

When they reached the motel, no other cars were in the parking lot but several linen carts were stationed in front of rooms as the maids went in and out, making beds and emptying wastebaskets. Colin pulled into the space in front of number twelve, turned off the engine and slumped in the seat. 'Oh thank you, Lord,' he said, letting his eyes close.

'I'll see if they've finished your room yet.' Mandy got out and walked to the window of Colin's room, cupping her hands beside her eyes as she looked through the glass. 'They have.'

Colin remained in his seat, his arms limp at his sides.

'Colin?'

'What.'

'They've done your room.'

After a few more moments he got out of the car, removed his wallet for the plastic card, which he inserted into the slot in the door, pushing it open.

'Should I come in?' Mandy said, still standing next to the window.

'I hope so.'

He waited as she went into the room ahead of him. 'If you can believe it,' she said, 'yesterday was the first time I've been in one of these rooms. I always come over here to visit Joanie, but I'd never been inside a room before.'

Colin came in after her. 'There's some coffee there,' he said, pointing at a tray on the bureau, with a pot on it and packets of coffee in a cup.

'Do you want any?' she said.

He closed the door. 'I thought you might.'

'I just drink coffee at work,' she said. 'Right now I'm too happy to have any.' She walked over to look at a picture on the wall. 'Are you happy?'

'Generally speaking.'

'Why are you happy,' she said.

'Why?'

'Maybe there's no reason.'

'I'm sure there is,' he said, 'if I gave it some thought.'

'Maybe just because it's a beautiful day.'

'That,' he said, 'and the fact that we aren't lying in adjoining drawers in a morgue. It's the little things that cheer me.'

'Could I ask you something,' Mandy said, folding her leg underneath herself as she sat down in a chair in the corner of the room, 'because you seem really . . .' She looked up at the ceiling. '. . . I don't know what you'd call it, the way you seem to me.'

It was quiet in the room as she thought.

'I'm afraid I can't help you.'

'Like someone who wouldn't get mad at me,' she said, looking back down at him. 'No matter what I would say. No matter what I would do.'

He shrugged. 'I don't suppose I would.'

'You wouldn't, would you.'

'You don't seem like someone anyone would get mad at.'

'Tell that to my family members,' she said, getting up again. She walked over to the window. There was a clicking sound as a maid wheeled her cart past on the walkway outside. 'Can I close the curtain?'

'Go ahead.'

Mandy reached to the side of the window and pulled a cord, drawing the curtain closed. 'I want to do something I've never done before,' she said, turning around. 'Okay?'

'Something you've never done before.'

'Is that okay?'

'Well what is it.'

'I don't want to talk about it,' she said. 'I just want to do it.'

'In your life you've never done it before?'

'Never.'

'Well I don't know,' Colin said, after a pause. 'Maybe you should try it out somewhere else first.'

'I want to do it here.' Starting at the top, she began to unfasten the buttons of her shirt.

Colin watched till she'd unfastened most of them down the front. 'Unbutton your shirt?' he said.

'What?'

'You've never unbuttoned your shirt before in your life?'

She finished unfastening them. 'Not for the reason I'm doing it now,' she said, as she slipped her arms out of the sleeves and set the shirt on the bureau. 'I've taken my clothes off with people for other reasons.' She put her hand between her breasts to undo the clasp of her bra. 'But not for this one.'

Colin watched her remove her bra to set on the bureau too. 'Which is what.'

Mandy bent down to untie her shoes, took them off, then straightened up and unbuckled her belt. 'This may sound strange,' she said, pushing her pants down around her legs, 'but with you I don't even feel self-conscious.'

'The thing you've never done,' he said.

She pushed her light-blue underwear down over her legs, then stepped out of both pairs of pants, leaving them on the carpet. 'This feels wonderful.' She stretched her arms up over her head toward the ceiling.

'Mandy.'

'The thing I've never done before.'

'If I might hear that now.'

'All right,' she said, raising herself up on her toes, 'ever since I was a little girl, whenever I was really happy, I'd want to take off my clothes. It's just always been an uncontrollable urge.' She lowered her arms till they were stretched out beside her. 'And when I was really young I'd just go ahead and start taking them off. But obviously people would be shocked and punish me and all that.' She came down from her toes and spread her feet apart on the carpet. 'So I learned to go to my room when I felt really happy and take them off by myself, away from other people.' Keeping her arms out beside herself she let her head fall backwards. 'And that's what I've always done.' She bent all the way forward, putting her fingers down on the floor to balance herself. 'Till today. This is the first time I've ever taken my clothes off for joy in front of another human being.'

Colin watched as she put her hands on top of her bare feet.

'And it's so much better this way. Because when you go in your room by yourself, sure, you might be expressing your joy, but there's that little guilty part, because you know you had to go off by yourself to do it, so the joy isn't quite complete.' She rose up to a standing position again, stretching her arms over her head.

'Incomplete joy,' Colin said.

'That's how it's always been before.'

He sat looking at her as she held perfectly still for a few seconds, looking back at him.

'Try it yourself if you want.'

'What's that.'

'What I'm doing.'

'Undressing for joy.'

'It's nothing to do with sex.'

'No.'

'If that's what you were thinking.'

'I wasn't.'

'Most men would think it was to do with that,' she said, slowly twisting from side to side with her arms out beside her, 'but I can tell you're a person who's able to just accept it for what it is. That's why I feel comfortable enough to do it in front of you.' She spun around in a circle. 'But really. Take yours off. It feels wonderful.'

He watched her spin around several more times. 'You know something,' he said, seating himself on the edge of the bed, 'actually I may take some of them off.'

'Don't just take some of them off. Take them all off.'

'I don't know if I'm as joyful as you are yet.'

'You will be, once they're off.'

Colin bent forward to untie his shoes.

'People have sex with their clothes on,' she said, raising a leg and taking hold of her foot with one of her hands. 'It happens all the time.'

Colin removed his shoes, and then his socks.

'You probably have yourself.'

'Had sex with my clothes on.'

'Have you?'

'I have, actually.' He unfastened the top button of his trousers.

'So have I,' she said. 'So what.'

'So what,' he repeated.

'Two people who are naked together don't have to have sex,' she said, 'any more than two people with their clothes on are necessarily not going to have it.'

'Naked people may have it more,' Colin said. 'I don't know if there have been studies.'

'I'm sure they do, but that's not my point.'

He took off his trousers. 'No, I understand your point. You're saying people with their clothes off don't have to.'

'Exactly.'

'I'm following your thinking.'

'I mean in a way it does kind of seem like we might,' she said. 'Does it seem that way to you?'

'Have sex.'

'What do you think.'

'I feel it could go either way.'

'This may sound odd,' she said, 'but if we do, maybe we should put our clothes back on.'

'Back on.'

'Get dressed again,' she said.

'To have sex.'

'If we do have it.'

'Why would we get dressed again.'

'So we wouldn't spoil the feeling of joy.'

'Oh.'

'Sex is one kind of joy,' she said, 'but I'm talking about the innocent kind of joy we're feeling now.'

Colin looked down at his trousers on the carpet.

'Why take the chance of spoiling that,' she said.

'And then take them back off again afterwards?'

'What?'

'I'm just asking – after we had sex, we'd then take our clothes back off again?'

'Don't you wear underpants?' she said, making large circles beside herself with her arms.

'I was in a rush when I left. I couldn't find clean ones.'

'I don't know about you,' Mandy said, 'but I'm starting to feel cold.' She walked around to the other side of the bed and pulled down the covers. 'Joanie and Fisher must be trying to save on their heating bill.' She got into the bed and pulled the covers up over herself.

Colin remained seated on the edge. 'Will we be putting our shoes back on to have sex?'

'You know that kind of innocent joy I was talking about?' she said. 'One thing about it, you never know when it's going to come, and you never know when it's going to vanish. It's magical.'

Colin nodded.

'So it may have gone for now,' she said, 'but that doesn't mean it won't be back. When we least expect it.' She moved under the covers over next to him. 'And in the meantime, while we're waiting for it to come back, we have the other kind.'

'The uninnocent kind.'

'Are you going to get into bed?'

'I have no idea.'

After a moment she reached up and began massaging his scalp with the tips of her fingers. 'Remember when I was doing this yesterday?'

'I do.'

'Did you like it?'

'Very much,' he said. 'It was planning for my Journey at the same time that sort of detracted.'

'Do you want to come in bed and I'll do it some more?' He raised himself up and she pulled down the covers on his side of the bed. 'Now you can get in.'

Colin got into the bed.

'Don't you want to take this off?' She began unbuttoning his shirt, then helped him remove it and dropped it on to the floor on his side of the bed.

'I may not quite have the basic concept yet.'

'What concept.'

'Co-ordinating the different types of joy with the various stages of clothes removal.'

She put her arm around his shoulders. 'You don't have the concept yet,' she said, one of her breasts coming to rest against the side of his face as she began moving her fingers through his hair again, 'but I can tell you why you don't.'

'Why is that.'

'You're trying to make it too complicated.'

'I've been told I do that.'

Both breasts covered his face as she reached around to massage the back of his head.

'It just clicked into place.'

She pulled back. 'I didn't hear you.'

'I said, it just clicked into place.'

'What did.'

'The basic concept.'

She looked down at him for a few moments. 'Colin?'

'Yes.'

'Do you like the way my breasts feel against your face?'

'It's a peaceful feeling.'

'Shall I put them there again?'

'If you're up to it.'

She leaned forward so they rested against his face again. 'I should have done this yesterday. Instead of making you think of beaches and forests.'

Colin closed his eyes and they sat quietly as she pressed against him.

'Too bad I can't get them to feel peaceful this way over at the Shores,' she said, 'but somehow I don't think I'd have my job too long.'

'I'm sure I can find a job for you in my organisation if they make you redundant.'

After a few more moments she pulled back again to look at him. 'Make me what?'

'Redundant.'

She frowned.

'You don't say that.'

'I never heard of it.'

'Fired?'

'Oh, fired.' She brought his head back against her breasts and again it was quiet.

Colin let his eyes close.

'Redundant,' she said. 'I thought that meant over and over again, something like that.'

'Actually,' Colin said, 'I think it might be one of those words that means pretty much anything you want it to.'

6

Ordinarily in doing a portrait Colin would choose his own subject. Something would strike him about someone he saw – a look in the eye, an expressive mouth – and he would approach the individual and ask if they would sit for him. He rarely made exceptions to this rule, although in the case of Mandy's brother he did, since no graceful way to decline the offer of Rob Martin as a subject came readily to mind.

The drawing was done on Saturday morning at Rob's high school. There were no classes in session, but a few students were walking around the paths and one of them directed Colin to the building containing the swimming pool, which is where they had planned to meet.

The pool filled nearly the whole interior of the low building, and as soon as Colin stepped inside he could see a large teenage boy doing the butterfly stroke, lurching from one end of the pool to the other, loudly sucking in air each time his head came out of the water. The next time he reached the shallow end Colin was squatting at the edge of the water beside the handles of an aluminium ladder.

'Rob?'

Grinning, the boy stood up and pushed a pair of goggles up over his forehead. 'Mandy's friend,' he said, struggling to catch his breath.

Colin reached out and shook his wet hand. 'Colin,' he said. 'Aren't I interrupting your practice?'

'I'm just messing around.'

Colin straightened up. They looked at each other a moment longer, then Colin glanced at a row of windows running along the top of the wall behind them. 'I was looking at the lighting,' he said. 'It's indirect, but I think we can work with it.' He set down his case several yards back from the pool.

'What do you want me to do.'

'Stand right there in the pool.' Colin removed his pad and a few pencils from the wooden case. 'Unless you'll be cold.'

'I never get cold.'

Colin looked down at his subject, waist deep in the water. 'Can you come this way a little?' He pointed at a broad black line on the bottom of the pool. 'Why don't you stand there.' Rob walked over and placed his feet on it. 'Perfect.'

'What about my goggles.'

'Leave them on. I like them.'

Rob reached up to adjust the small pair of goggles strapped around the top of his head. 'They're my lucky goggles,' he said, lowering his arm. 'Coach wore them in Sydney during the Olympics.'

'Oh?' Colin said, taking a step back. 'Your coach was in the Olympics?'

'Not in them exactly. He went over to Sydney as a trainer. While he was there he bought a bunch of goggles and put each of them on and off in the Olympic Village so he could hand them out as souvenirs over the years to his top swimmers. It's amazing the incentive it gives you to own something that was actually worn over there.'

Colin put all but one of his pencils in his shirt pocket and turned back the cover of his sketch pad.

Rob raised his hand. 'Sir?'

'You don't need to call me sir, Rob.'

'Could I say something before you start?'

'Of course.'

'I don't know if Mandy mentioned I'm pretty heavily into the Lord.'

Colin nodded. 'She did.'

'Is there some way you could have that come across in the drawing?'

'Being heavily into the Lord.'

'I mean I don't know how you would,' Rob said, slapping the top of the water. 'You're the artist. But I just wish you could.'

'I'll do my best.'

'Maybe convey sort of a feeling of inner happiness, something like that.'

'An inner light,' Colin said.

'That's it.'

'I'll try, Rob, that's all I can do.' Colin raised the pad in front of himself.

'The two things I want to come through in the picture,' Rob said, holding up two fingers, 'are one, that I'm a Christian, and two, that I'm a swimmer.'

'I understand that, Rob. Don't you want to put a towel around your shoulders while we do this, to keep warm?'

'I'm blessed with fabulous circulation.'

Colin made several circling motions over the pad with his pencil, then sketched the outline of Rob's head.

'Not to bring up a painful subject or anything, but I heard your girlfriend over in England just gave you the heave-ho.'

As Colin began drawing his ears, Rob cupped his hand and hit the surface of the pool, sending some water up over the opposite side.

'Rob.'

'You want me to hold still.'

'You can splash,' Colin said, 'as long as you keep turned this way.' He began drawing Rob's nose.

'What happened,' Rob said. 'She got sucked into a cult or something?'

'What's that.'

'Your girlfriend. Mandy said she might have gotten sucked into a cult.'

'It crossed my mind at first. But in retrospect I can see I was just very distraught when I thought of that.'

Rob slapped some more water toward the side of the pool. 'Satan's amazing,' he said, 'isn't he?'

Moving forward slightly, Colin squinted at Rob's mouth.

'One minute you're just going along, leading an ordinary life. Everything's normal. Then whoosh! He creeps up behind you and sucks you into a cult.'

'As I said, Rob, I don't think that's what happened any more.'

'What do you think did happen.'

He sketched in Rob's chin. 'In a word,' he said, 'I'm afraid she just got tired of me.' He removed the pencils from the pocket of his shirt, selected a new one and returned the others. 'It was a very long-term relationship. I'm afraid it finally just collapsed of its own weight.'

'It wasn't faith-based, doesn't sound like,' Rob said.

'Wasn't what?'

'The relationship. It doesn't sound like it was based on the strength of Christ.'

'It wasn't.'

The rest of the portrait was done in silence, with Rob periodically flicking his fingers against the water, but at all times keeping his face forward.

Finally Colin held the drawing out at arm's length to study.

'Finished?' Rob said.

Colin nodded.

'Mind if I have a look?'

'I want you to.' He quickly added another line to the side of his head as Rob climbed out of the pool and walked up beside him. Colin held it in front of them so they both could see it. 'What do you think.'

Rob nodded. 'It looks like me.'

'I think so.'

'The eyes,' Rob said, pointing, 'that's definitely how my eyes look.'

'Careful.'

Rob pulled back his dripping arm.

'I'm glad you feel I captured your eyes,' Colin said. 'When the eyes are right, usually everything else falls into place.'

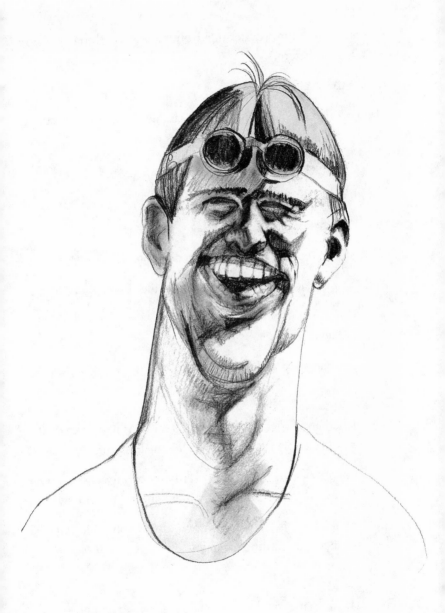

'The only thing I'm wondering,' Rob said, 'is the thing we were talking about before.'

'What's that.'

'The two things,' Rob said. 'The swimmer, and the Christian. Okay, the goggles. That shows the swimmer.'

'Definitely,' Colin said.

'But what about the other.'

'Your inner happiness,' Colin said.

Rob nodded, keeping his eyes on the drawing.

'Well I think that comes through in the smile,' Colin said. 'To me, the smile reflects the inner light.'

They studied it together.

'In a way I guess it does,' Rob said.

'I think so.'

Rob reached up to wiggle a finger in his ear. 'But I don't know if a person would exactly get a Christian feeling from it.'

'To be honest,' Colin said, 'that's a difficult quality to convey in pencil. Communicating spirituality in graphite is never easy.'

'And don't take this the wrong way either,' Rob said, 'but you may have made me smiling *too* much.'

'Oh?'

'For a Christian it should be more like a glowing feeling.'

'I think you glow.'

'Look, here's an idea,' Rob said, 'what about drawing a little crucifix on a chain around my neck. I have one at home. It's just not
on at the moment.'

Colin looked at his drawing in silence a few moments. 'I try to
exclude material objects as much as possible,' he said finally. 'They
distract us from the subject's personality.' He gestured with his pencil
at the page. 'The goggles work, but from the point-of-view of balance
I don't think the composition will support another physical object.'

'It's a tiny crucifix.'

'That may be, but it's going to pull attention away from the face.'

'But it would show my commitment.'

'I realise that, but it would also clutter the composition.'

A large drop of water fell on the page as Rob stepped forward and
pointed at the drawing of his neck. 'Just put it there. Actually,
that's going to make the composition even better.'

'How so, Rob.'

'Because then you'll have the goggles *and* the cross. That shows my
whole personality. So the composition will be perfect.'

Colin watched the spot on one of Rob's cheeks grow larger and
darken as it was absorbed by the paper.

'Sorry about that.'

'It'll dry,' Colin said, closing the pad. 'Listen, why don't you give
the crucifix to your sister. Have her bring it to the motel and I'll
see if there's a way to work it in.'

'Bless you, sir.'

7

When the small blue car turned into the motel entrance and stopped in front of the office, Joanie was going through her credit card receipts from the day before, adding them up again to confirm that no errors had been made. She glanced through the window at the woman stepping out of the car, but then turned her eyes down to the calculator again till the woman had come into the office and was standing on the other side of the counter. Then she looked up and smiled. 'I'm afraid we're all booked for tonight.'

'I'm looking for one of your guests,' the woman said in an English accent. 'I don't need a room.'

It was quiet as the two of them smiled at each other across the counter.

'What guest would that be.'

'A Colin Ware.'

'Ware,' Joanie repeated, after another couple of seconds had passed.

The woman nodded, then again for a few moments it was quiet.

'Well let me just look in our register. I'll see if we have anyone here by that name.'

'Thank you.'

Joanie turned the large book around in front of her. She flipped back a few pages, moving her head down slightly to read some of the entries, running her finger along underneath them as she read.

'Colin, you said.'

'I believe he arrived last Monday.'

'Of last week.'

'Yes. Not yesterday.'

Joanie continued looking through the book, studying the pages, turning them backward, then forward again.

'There can't be that many new guests just for that one day, can there,' the woman said.

'No,' Joanie said, placing her finger on one of the entries, 'and here he is.'

'You found him.'

'I did.'

'And is he still here.'

'Is he still here.' Joanie began turning the pages forward again. 'Is Mr Ware still here. Let's just see if Mr Ware is still here at the inn.' Looking at the most recent page, Joanie pursed her lips a moment, then nodded. 'Yes. He still is.'

'Good. And may I ask which room he's in.'

'Which room,' Joanie said. 'Which room, which room.' The blond woman across from her waited as Joanie again flipped back through the pages of the register. 'I believe my husband was the one who checked Mr Ware in and I may have to touch base with him to be sure exactly where he put him.'

'Your husband didn't make a note of which room he put him in?'

'Ordinarily he would have,' Joanie said, 'but this time of year, because of all the tourists, sometimes we'll switch people around – someone might prefer a corner room, someone else might not want to be next to the ice machine—'

'What can all that have to do with your husband checking him in.'

'Twelve,' Joanie said, nodding. 'Yes. Mr Ware is in twelve. I do know who you mean now that I think of it. Is he a British gentleman?'

'Yes.'

Joanie nodded. 'I believe I do know who that is.'

'And he's in room twelve.'

'Yes.'

'Thank you.' She started toward the door.

'But he's not there now.'

The woman stopped.

'Now that I remember who he is,' Joanie said, 'I did notice him going out a little while ago. But let's be sure.' She picked up the receiver of the phone and held it out to her. 'You take this, just in case I'm mistaken.' The woman put the receiver to her ear as Joanie pressed two buttons on the keypad. 'But I've been right here and I'm sure I haven't seen him come back.'

'He's not there,' the woman said, handing back the receiver.

'If you give me your name,' Joanie said, hanging it up, 'I'll put on his message light so he'll know the minute he gets back you were here.'

'I'd rather wait,' the woman said.

'Wait?'

'For him to come back,' she said. 'Do you have to be a guest to sit out by the pool?'

'Not if you're visiting a registered guest.'

'So I may wait.'

'Oh yes.'

She left the office, opened the door of her car to remove a bag from the front seat, then walked to the low fence enclosing the pool and went through its gate, past several children who were swimming, and to a chair in the corner.

Joanie watched her through the window till she was seated, then picked up the phone again and pressed one of the buttons. 'Come here.' She hung up and looked back out at the woman, who was reaching into her bag to remove a pack of cigarettes.

A door at the rear of the office opened and Fisher looked in. 'What's up.'

'Come over here.'

Fisher walked across the office and stopped next to his wife, who was pointing out the window. 'The woman by the pool,' she said. 'In the chair by the deep end.'

He looked out at her. She'd put the cigarette between her lips and was holding a lighter to the end of it.

'What does she think she's doing.'

'Not the cigarette, Fisher.'

A grey-haired guest got up from his towel and stepped over to her. Joanie and her husband watched as he spoke to the woman, indicating a sign on the fence, then as the woman took a deep drag from the cigarette before grinding it out on the cement in front of her chair.

'That's Vera,' Joanie said.

'Vera.'

'Colin's Vera.'

'Who?'

'Wake up, Fisher.' She snapped her fingers in his face. 'The one he came over here to escape.'

'Oh good Lord.'

They watched as the woman folded her hands on the bag in her lap.

'Are you sure?'

'She was just in the office.'

'And told you that's who she is?'

The woman tipped her face up to the sun and closed her eyes.

'She has an English accent. She's here asking for Colin. Come on, Fisher, who else could it be.'

'Maybe it was an Australian accent. Those are tricky to tell apart.'

'How likely is it that an Australian woman is going to show up asking for Colin Ware.'

'Canadian?'

'Fisher, I'm not going to stand here while you go through the British Empire. It is her.'

They watched as Vera reached up to brush a fly away from her face.

'Go out and talk to her,' Joanie said.

He remained where he was.

'Fisher?'

'Joanie, I have nothing to say to the woman.'

'Just try to draw her out. We've got to find out what she's up to.'

Again the two of them stood silently side-by-side watching Vera sun herself.

'This really isn't our business, Joanie.'

'Of course it is.'

'How.'

'Because Mandy Martin's been living here with Colin for the past week and the woman who wrecked his life, who drove him five thousand miles over here, is sitting out by our swimming pool. Don't tell me all hell isn't going to break loose when they come tootling back in here.'

'There's an outside chance of that.'

'Outside,' she said, turning toward him. 'Fisher, when yellow police tape is wrapped around the motel, and we're splashed all over the front page of the *Banner*, and no one will come within a hundred miles of this place, maybe then you'll realise it might have been a good idea to do something.'

Still Fisher stood where he was, looking out at Vera.

'Fisher! Why aren't you going out there!'

'The woman belongs to a cult, Joanie.'

'What?'

'The innocent little conversation you were just having with her?' He shook his head. 'I won't even try to guess how many subliminal messages came in under your radar.'

115

'Oh my God in heaven.' Joanie came out from behind the counter. 'Cover the desk.'

He stepped in front of her. 'Joanie,' he said. 'I've read accounts about this stuff by professional deprogrammers that would chill your blood. You are a babe in the woods.' He pushed open the door. 'Stay here.'

Fisher walked to the pool, nodding to a sunbathing guest as he entered the fenced enclosure. Then he picked up an empty aluminium chair and carried it over to set down beside Vera.

She lowered her head and opened her eyes as he seated himself.

'I'm the co-manager,' he said. 'That was my wife Joanie you spoke to in the office.'

'Is Colin back?' Vera twisted her head around to look over at the rooms.

Fisher leaned forward. He picked up the cigarette butt from beside the leg of her chair and set in the palm of his hand.

'There was no ashtray.'

'No problem,' Fisher said.

A young boy jumped off the side of the pool, tucked in his knees and hit the water, splashing a woman lying on her towel.

'No more of that,' Fisher said when he came up.

He swam away.

'Mr Ware isn't back yet, is he,' Vera said.

'No.' Fisher sat looking down at the crushed cigarette in his cupped hand.

'Do you mind if I wait here for him?'

'Not at all.'

Vera watched him a few more moments, then tilted her face up to the sun again.

'But as long as we're speaking of Mr Ware – Colin – he did my portrait last week.'

She looked back down at him. 'Oh?'

'Very nice,' Fisher said, nodding. 'I thought it came out very well.'

'He's an excellent artist.'

'Yes. Excellent.' Fisher cleared his throat and it was quiet for a moment or two except for the noise of the other guests. 'Vera's your name then?' he said at last.

'It would seem he mentioned me,' she said after a moment.

'We chatted as he worked.'

'I hate to imagine what he said.'

'We just talked casually.' Fisher reached down to wave his fingers back and forth across the spot on the cement and disperse the black specks from where Vera had ground out the cigarette. 'Are you alone then?' he said when he was finished.

'Sorry?'

'Did you enter the country by yourself?'

'Yes.'

'Are you sure?

She frowned.

'All right,' he said, 'I'll take your word for it.'

'Who else would be with me.' When he didn't respond, Vera looked down at the cement beside her chair. 'Oh,' she said after a few moments, 'my new husband.'

'Your new husband,' Fisher said, 'among others.'

'Others?'

Fisher nodded.

'What others.'

'Oh I wouldn't know that, would I. Other members possibly?' He raised his hand to attract the attention of a teenage girl in a bathing suit preparing to come through the gate. 'Miss? No glass in here.'

She looked at him a moment, then turned and walked away with her glass of Coke.

'Other members of what,' Vera said

'May I call you Vera?'

'Of course.'

'I thought you might have been given a different name.'

The woman in front of them got to her feet and picked up her towel.

'You what?' Vera said.

Fisher looked up at the sky. 'Let me think of the best way to put this.' It was silent a few moments, then he turned his eyes back down to the pool. 'Vera, I have a very wonderful wife – Joanie, you met her – who I have every intention of spending the rest of my life with, and we have a boy off at college that we're so darn proud of neither of us can stop bragging about him. In other words, we're a cohesive and loving nuclear family unit.'

Vera sat in the chair beside him, still looking down at the cement.

'And that's the way we're going to stay.'

Except for the children yelling and splashing in the pool, it was quiet again for a few moments before she spoke. 'You're going to remain a cohesive family unit,' she said finally.

'You bet we are.'

The woman finished folding her towel and walked away from them.

'Sir,' Vera said, 'you seem to have some reason for telling me all this.'

'You bet I do.'

'But I have no idea what it is.'

The large branch of a tree extended partially out over the pool overhead, and one of its orange leaves fluttered down between them.

'I'm just here to try and get things sorted with Colin.'

'So you say.'

'And forgive me,' she said, 'but you keep implying I have ulterior motives of some kind.'

'Vera,' he said, reaching down to pick up the leaf and put it in his hand with the cigarette butt, 'I'm going to let you in on a little saying we use here in America for situations like this, and it goes like this: "If the shoe fits, wear it".'

'That's used in England as well,' she said, 'but my point is I don't know what you're talking about.'

Fisher cleared his throat. 'Vera, does the word Swami mean anything to you?'

'Swami.'

'That's what I said.'

'Why would you ask me that.'

'Well because personally,' Fisher said, 'I wouldn't recognise one if he jumped up and bit me on the nose. But your experience with them may be different than mine.'

She turned toward him and for several seconds the two of them looked quietly at each other. 'It is,' she said finally.

'It is.'

'Yes, I haven't had a Swami do that to me.'

'It was a figure of speech, Vera.'

She nodded. 'I see. Well let's just hope it never happens.'

Again the two of them sat in silence, till Fisher looked at his watch. 'They're putting on a gay wedding reception out here by the pool this evening,' he said, scraping his chair back as he got to his feet. 'Staff will need my supervision setting up for that. And tomorrow we're getting ready for a flock of maple syrup conventioneers. So I can't give you any more of my time right now, Vera. Enjoy your day.' He walked past her and to the gate.

8

Mandy had moved into number twelve with Colin before returning to work. She'd invited him to stay at her apartment, but
Colin felt this would have been an irresponsible imposition on his
part, so she brought over the dress she wore at her job to put in the
motel closet, and when Monday morning came she drank two
cups of the powdered coffee from the tray on the bureau, put the
dress on and drove to Shining Shores.

At the end of Mandy's first day back at work, Colin was waiting
for her outside the entrance of the rest home, and this routine was
repeated the second day, although on that day she needed to go to

a nearby pharmacy to fill a prescription that one of the residents needed the next morning.

Standing at the rear of the drug store as the pharmacist counted out the tablets and put them in a container, Colin's attention was drawn to the man's face, and he found himself stepping closer to study his features as he placed a label on the container, put it in a small white sack and carried it out to Mandy.

After Mandy had received the pills, Colin introduced himself to the pharmacist, explaining quietly, since other customers were waiting, that if there were any chance of taking half an hour or so to do a sketch of him it would be a great honour for Colin and the drawing would be hung in an exhibition in Colin's London gallery, to which the pharmacist would be sent an invitation, a custom that Colin followed with all his subjects.

The pharmacist looked over at Mandy as Colin was talking, and after she nodded her endorsement agreed to let Colin do the drawing, even asking him to come behind the glass partition to do it as he worked.

After bringing his case and sketch pad in from Mandy's car, Colin began to draw, pausing each time the pharmacist had to carry an order out to a customer, assuring him when he came back that the interruptions weren't detracting from the quality of the work.

Because Mandy had begun to feel restless since returning to work and wanted to get away from familiar surroundings, they decided to go to a restaurant in another town to eat dinner. On the drive there Colin expressed a misgiving over whether the sketch pad he'd been sold the week before did in fact contain acid-free paper as he'd been told, and although Mandy asked him a few questions about acid-free paper it clearly wasn't a topic that fired her enthusiasm. However, she did want to see the sketch he'd done, so Colin brought the pad into the restaurant with them, and when the waiter had finished taking their orders and poured each of them a glass of wine, he opened the pad and leaned it against the wall at the side of the table.

Mandy studied the drawing without talking.

'I can tell you're a stern critic,' he said finally.

'I'm not a stern critic.'

'It looked like you were preparing to deliver a scathing review.'

'I guess you didn't have time to do his ears,' she said.

Colin picked up his glass and held it as he looked at the drawing.

'They're not there,' she said.

'I know.'

'I just wondered why.'

Colin set the glass down on the table without drinking from it.

'Maybe I shouldn't have asked.'

'You should have,' he said, 'it's just that I've just never defended my work exactly on this basis before.'

'Look, you don't have to defend your work to me, for God's sake.'

'I respect your judgement.'

'Well you shouldn't.'

'But sometimes it's difficult to translate visual things into verbal ways of saying them.'

'I guess you just didn't want to put them on there,' she said.

He nodded. 'There's the translation I was looking for.'

'Did he look at it?'

'The chemist? Yes.'

'What did you just call him?'

'Chemist,' Colin said. 'That seemed to be his profession.'

She shook her head. 'We don't call them that.'

'Pharmacist,' Colin said.

'Right.'

'He did see it.'

'Did he say anything about it?'

'He thought it was a good likeness.'

'Did he say anything about the ears?'

'No.'

'Because I would have if it was me.'

'What would you have said.'

'Put them on.'

It was quiet for a few moments as each of them looked at an empty table beside theirs.

'Can I say something, Mandy?'

'I'm not stopping you.'

He reached across their table to put his hand on hers. 'Now you said you wanted to drive all the way to a different town for dinner because you're starting to feel suffocated in New Cardiff.'

'I didn't say that.'

'What did you say.'

'Suffocated since I went back to work.'

'Whatever it was,' he said, ' the point is that you're sort of snapping at me tonight.'

'Look, put ears on him or don't put ears on him. Why do you ask me about it.'

'Mandy,' he said, squeezing her hand slightly, 'I don't really think it's the drawing that's bothering you.'

'Did you ever think something might be bothering you?' she said, looking up at him. 'Like the person you loved all your life suddenly gets married to someone else?'

'You feel I'm thinking about Vera.'

'Anyone would be.'

He looked down at a small vase of flowers at the side of the table. 'I agree. It seems like I would.'

'Of course.'

'But once the initial shock wore off . . .' He shrugged. 'It's like the time had come for things to end with Vera, and they did, unexpected though it was, but now it's over and I can see it's for the best and that's all there is to it.'

'Why is it for the best.'

'Because it is. And in the moments I was honest with myself – few and far between as they were – I think I'd already begun to recognise things had reached the point where the two of us were just going through the motions with each other.'

'Did you ever tell her that?'

'I tried.'

'And what did she say.'

'She'd laugh it off.' He looked back across the table at Mandy. 'But the point is you said I was bothered by thoughts of her and I'm really not.'

'Well nothing's bothering me either,' she said, pulling her hand out from under his, 'so why are we even talking about this.'

'May I suggest what I think's on your mind?'

'Nothing is.'

'But, Mandy, what about having someone drop into your life out of the blue – from a foreign country on top of everything else – and turn it upside-down. Might that not be slightly upsetting to you?'

'Not really,' she said. 'Anyway it's not a foreign country.'

'England,' he said.

'I know the country you're talking about.'

'I thought it was foreign.'

She shook her head.

'What is it.'

'You can't tell me why you left the ears off. I can't explain why England's not a foreign country.' He tried putting his hand on hers again but she rested it in her lap.

'Mandy.'

'I happen to be depressed at the moment,' she said. 'Don't you ever get depressed?'

'Yes, and when I do I try to work out why. And the reason you're depressed – one of them – is that I've come over here and scrambled your life up.'

'God, will you please stop saying that?' she said, looking across the table at him.

'But it's true.'

'I don't care. I'm asking you to stop saying it.'

They sat quietly a few moments looking at each other. 'Will you?'

'Of course.'

'Thank you.' She picked up her wine glass.

Colin picked up his own. 'Do you ever watch old movies,' he said.

'What old movies.'

'Any old movies. Black-and-white old movies.'

'What are you talking about this for.'

'Do you?'

'Why.'

'Just bear with me.'

'I've watched some.'

'Old World War Two movies. The old romantic ones with the war as a backdrop.'

She shook her head.

'You don't know those.'

'I don't know why we're talking about this all of a sudden.'

'I'm working up to a parallel.'

'Work up to it then.' She put down her glass.

'All right,' he said, 'let's say you have this Yank over in London. And he has an English sweetheart. She's a nurse, say. And the two of them are sitting in a canteen. In fact it looks a little like this place.'

'Colin.'

'Could you let me go on with this.'

'It's just stupid.'

'I know,' he said, putting down his own wine glass again, 'but there they are, sitting in the empty canteen together. The other soldiers and sailors have all left. The last musician puts away his trombone. An unbearably poignant moment.' Colin raised his hand. 'Now the scene changes. We're on a British hospital ship, on its way back from France.'

'Colin.'

'The war's been won. Home and hearth lie ahead as the ship makes its way across the Channel.'

'Colin,' she said again.

'But who's on the ship,' he said, 'lying in a bed, bandaged from head to toe.'

'Who.'

'The nurse's fiancé,' he said, 'an RAF pilot named – oddly enough – Colin, presumed lost in a daylight bombing raid over Stuttgart.'

'Are we finished talking about this yet,' she said.

'Yes.'

'What's the parallel.'

'It didn't work out. Give me your hand.'

'No.'

'I went off the track when you stopped me talking about the other subject.'

'Say what you want then!'

'You don't even have the sense of security any longer from being in your own apartment.'

'Yes, you've upset my life.'

'You acknowledge it.'

'What difference does it make,' she said, reaching up to wipe her eye with the back of her hand. 'My life's been upset since the minute I was born.'

'Do you ever think about my going back to England?' he said.

'Why should I think of that.' She looked away.

'Do you?'

'No.'

'Never?'

'Why should I,' she said again.

'Because I don't live in America,' he said, 'and I'm doing the drawings for an exhibition in London. So if for no other reason, I'll have to go back for that.'

Mandy took a deep breath.

'But you never think about that.'

'Colin, I do happen to have a few other things going on in my life besides you, you know.'

'I think about going back,' he said.

'I'm sure you do. You have to make plans.'

'Do you want to know what I think about it?'

'Not particularly.'

'That I don't want to.'

'Why not,' she said, after a moment.

'Why do you think, Mandy.'

She shrugged. 'I guess you like America.'

'I may like America,' he said, picking up his glass again, 'but that's not why I don't want to go back.'

'Why don't you then.'

'See if you can guess, Mandy.'

'Better weather here?'

'Try once more.'

'Because I'm here,' she said, making a face at him across the table.

'Good, Mandy.'

'What a great reason not to go back.' She wiped at her other eye.

'Oh I am going back,' he said.

'Obviously.'

'I have to.'

'So why are you bringing all this shit up,' she said, 'just to torture me?'

'I'm bringing it up because I don't want to go back alone.'

For a long time Mandy looked down at the red-and-white chequered tablecloth in front of her. 'What do you mean by that,' she said finally.

'Just what I said.'

'You don't want to go back by yourself?'

'That's right.'

Again it was quiet. 'I don't . . . you mean you want to take some-one with you?'

'Only if they want to come,' he said. 'I don't plan to tie them up and kidnap them.'

She shut her eyes tightly, then opened them again. A tear rolled down one of her cheeks and fell on to the tablecloth. 'Sorry.'

'Oh sure, I'd tie them up and kidnap them if I could, but the air-lines have got so nit-picking about hand luggage lately . . .'

'So who is this person,' she said, still not looking up. She reached for the salt shaker, held it a moment, but then returned it to the table.

'That I'd like to take back with me?'

'I'd be sort of curious.' She moved her hand toward the salt shaker again, but before it got there he took hold of it.

'Only one guess this time,' he said.

She shook her head.

'You want more?'

'I don't want any.'

'None?'

She sat looking down at their two hands, resting on the tablecloth beside the flowers in the vase. 'I'm afraid I'll be wrong.'

'You won't be.'

'How do you know that if you don't know what my guess is.'

'I do.'

She looked slowly up at him. 'What.'

He shook his head.

'You're not saying?'

'No.'

'Why not.'

For a long time they sat looking at each other across the table. Then finally Colin raised his glass. 'Cheers, Mandy.'

When they got back to the motel, lights had been set up around the pool and there was a crowd of people in the enclosure. 'What's all that,' Colin said, pulling into the space in front of their room.

'They do wedding receptions here.'

He stopped and they got out of the car, then stood looking over toward the pool.

The married couple was standing at the far end next to a multi-tiered cake on a table, while a photographer crouched in front of them, his bulb flashing as they fed each other a piece of cake. 'Is that a custom here?' Colin said, as the guests applauded and cheered. 'Mutual cake feeding?'

'They want us to have some,' Mandy said.

Someone was holding up two pieces of cake on small paper plates and looking over at them.

'We never did have dessert tonight.'

They walked across the parking lot to the pool and the guest handed the cake over the top of the low fence to them. 'Thank you,' Colin said, taking his, 'be sure and give our congratulations to the couple.'

'I'll get you some champagne.' The guest turned and walked back among the others.

Mandy picked up a tiny plastic fork from the edge of her plate and cut a little piece. 'Pretty nice of them,' she said, raising it to her mouth.

'Very nice of them.' Colin took a bite of his.

'Lemon,' Mandy said.

'Lemon cake?'

'I think so.'

'I think you're right.'

They ate another few bites.

'Good,' Mandy said.

Colin nodded. 'Moist.'

'I noticed that – it does taste moist.'

By the time the guest returned they'd finished the cake, and they handed the paper plates back to him over the fence as he gave them their champagne glasses.

'You really shouldn't be doing this,' Colin said, as he took his.

'They want you to share in their joy,' the guest said. 'I told them you wished them well.'

'Yes we do.'

Mandy took a swallow of her champagne.

'Are the two of you from England?'

'He is. I'm from New Cardiff.'

When they returned to the room, Mandy was the first to go in. 'The message light's flashing,' she said, walking toward the phone on the bedside table. 'I'll see what it is.'

'I know what it is.' Colin came in and closed the door. 'They want me to pay.'

'You haven't paid yet?' Mandy said, putting her hand on the phone.

'For tonight I have. But they like people to pay in advance this time of year because it's so busy.'

She looked down at the blinking light. 'You're sure that's it?'

'It happened before.'

'Don't pay before you have to.' She removed her hand from the phone. 'It sounds like they're getting greedy.' She continued looking down at the flashing red light. 'How do you turn this thing off.'

'They have to do it from the office.'

She reached toward the phone again.

'But let me worry about it in the morning,' Colin said, walking into the bathroom. 'Just leave it for now.'

'It's annoying.'

'Cover it up.'

'With what.'

He turned the water on in the sink. 'Anything.'

She watched it blink a few more times, then pulled out the drawer in the table. It was empty except for a Bible. She removed it, opened it in the middle and placed it upside down over the telephone.

Part II

9

When the knock came on his door the next morning Colin had just finished his shower. 'One second,' he called from the bathroom. Quickly he dried off his back and legs, wrapping the large towel tightly around his waist and tucking it in as he went through the doorway to his room and to his trousers draped over the chair. He removed some notes from his wallet and carried them to the door, opening it and raising the money up toward Vera.

She was standing holding her bag, and except for her eyes once moving to glance past him into the room she remained looking back at him quietly, without changing her expression. 'Hello,' she said finally.

Very slowly he lowered the money.

'Colin, it's not going to be smooth. There's no use pretending anything either of us can say will prevent this from being the most awkward moment we've ever had.'

'Vera,' he whispered, after another few seconds had passed.

This time she looked past him and at several different places in his room before turning her eyes back to Colin's. 'So. I'll just jump in. I'll just . . .' She moved her bag to her other hand. 'Jeremy. He's the one who told me you were here. He said you rang him at the end of last week. I guess you asked him to tell your parents where you were – and I can understand perfectly why you didn't have him notify me, but he knew how worried I was so he . . .'

Colin looked toward the office. Behind the desk Joanie was leaning slightly to the side to see out the window.

'By the way, Jeremy did mention he's giving you a show in the spring – of the drawings you're doing here – so at least something positive's coming out of all this.' Vera glanced back at the office as Joanie stepped quickly out of sight. 'And it doesn't make this any easier to be spied on by your extremely odd managers.' She turned so she could get between Colin and the side of the doorway and go into the room. 'What is wrong with those two people?'

Colin watched as she walked over to stand by the unmade bed.

'Do you know?'

For a long time he stood looking at her in silence.

'Please talk, Colin.'

'Roger Pelham,' he said.

She nodded. 'Roger Pelham,' she repeated.

'Where is he.'

'We do need to talk about Roger.'

'Is he here?'

'Well that seems a little self-evident.'

'In America.'

'Will you close the door so I can tell you?'

Colin closed the door.

'No,' she said.

'He's not in America.'

'No.'

'Well where is he.'

She glanced around the room. 'No ashtrays, obviously.' She walked to the chair, removed his trousers from its seat and put them over its arm. 'The first thing we should do is just stand back from our emotions. That's what you always say. And that's what we should do now.'

'Are you married to Roger Pelham?'

'I want to answer that in full,' she said, 'that's why I'm here.'

'In full.'

'Colin,' she said, seating herself, 'I have absolutely nothing to say in my defence. I've behaved disgracefully and I'm prepared to accept society's judgement.'

'What's that supposed to mean.'

'What it means, Colin.'

He looked down at a pillow resting in the centre of the bed. 'Did you do something to him? Something terrible?'

'Like kill him? Not exactly.' She opened her bag, removed a pack of cigarettes but then returned it and snapped the bag shut again.

'You didn't exactly kill him.'

'No.'

'Buried him alive? What.'

'Colin, have you had breakfast yet.'

'Breakfast.'

'I'll get us breakfast. It's the least I can do.'

'What did you do to the man.'

'Nothing.'

'Stand him up?'

'I'm a little afraid to tell you,' she said. 'I didn't expect the red carpet treatment over here, but I did think the fact that I've travelled five thousand miles to say sorry might soften your heart toward me enough so you could at least sit down while I told you.'

'Say sorry?'

She nodded. 'Yes,' she said, 'I've come to apologise.'

'For putting me through what you did.'

She nodded.

'Then backing out of the wedding?'

'Not exactly.'

'Vera, don't keep saying that.'

'I didn't back out of the wedding.'

'He did then.'

'No.'

'Well there's you and there's him, that pretty much exhausts the possibilities.'

After a few moments had passed Vera touched the end of one of her fingers to her tongue and bent forward to rub at a small spot on the toe of her shoe. 'There was never a Roger Pelham,' she said, removing the spot.

'Never what?'

'Courage, Vera.' She looked up at the ceiling. 'The moment is here. The one you've been dreading night and day. The one that's been keeping you awake for a week. The one that even a flight across the Atlantic with two movies and five *Marie Claires* couldn't put out of your mind. Courage.'

'Vera.'

She kept her eyes fixed on a point above his head. 'I deserve it, Colin. Don't hold back.'

'Could you look at me please, Vera?'

She waited a moment, then lowered her eyes.

147

'What are you talking about?'

'Well I mean I'm sure there are hundreds of Roger Pelhams walking around. Thousands no doubt, including in America and the other English-speaking countries.'

'But none that you know?'

'No.'

He stood for a long time holding the money at his side and looking at her, then he turned his eyes down to the carpet and finally up to her again.

'Has it registered yet,' she said.

'No Roger Pelhams that you know.'

'You haven't quite got it yet. Let's see.' She spent several moments clearing her throat. 'I'll have to plunge straight in. First of all, I am not going to try and put it down to Alicia.' She held up her hand. 'It will seem as though I am. But I'm not. Yes, it was all her idea. Yes, she kept prodding me forward when I wasn't sure – which I never was, right from the beginning. You're going to think I'm trying to shift the blame because I point out that she was the mastermind behind it all, but I'm not trying to shift it.' Vera placed her hand on her chest. 'At the end of the day, I am responsible for the whole sordid thing. If I didn't know that I wouldn't be here now. Would I.'

Slowly Colin sat down on the bed. 'Oh God, Vera.'

'Just because Alicia was the one who thought up the invitation, and went down and had it printed up, and took it to the post office and mailed it, does not absolve me. And I fully realise that.'

Colin picked up the pillow from beside him and put it on his lap. 'A joke,' he said.

'Not exactly.'

'Vera,' he said, holding up his hand in her direction but not looking at her.

'All right, yes. It was a joke.' She nodded. 'But let's look more deeply here at who the joke was on. Now we both know how jealous Alicia is of our relationship. We've said that many times.'

'A joke.'

'Please let me finish, Colin.'

'A joke,' he said again, shaking his head and looking down at the pillow.

'So what has happened here,' she said, 'is that in that jealous little brain of hers, Alicia came up with this prank to try and torpedo your and my relationship. And stupid trusting big sister that I am, I took the whole thing at face value and went along thinking you and I would have a good laugh when it was all over, never imagining . . .'

Colin put his finger up to his lips. 'Vera.'

'Yes, Colin, what.'

'Shhh.'

'Right,' she said, nodding. 'Sorry.'

'How did you get here,' he said.

'I flew.'

'No. Here.' He pointed down at the rug.

149

'Your motel? I drove here.'

'In what.'

'I rented a car,' she said, 'yesterday when I got in.'

'At the airport?'

'JFK.'

'And drove up to New Cardiff.'

She nodded.

'How was it,' he said. 'How was the drive.'

'Beautiful. Incredible colours of the leaves.'

'Are you staying locally?' Colin said.

Vera got up from her chair. 'Yes I am.' She removed a small card from her bag and carried it over to Colin. 'This is my motel.'

Without looking at it he took it and set it down on the bed.

'The Cardiff Arms,' she said, walking back toward her chair. 'A pretentious name, but slightly less sterile than most things American. They've made a little waterfall out the back you listen to as you're falling—'

'Vera?'

'Yes, Colin.'

'Don't sit down again.'

She stopped in front of the chair. It was quiet a few moments, then she turned around. 'Colin.'

'Just go, Vera.' He pointed toward the door. 'Please.'

'Colin,' she said, 'if you could have seen me after you disappeared.'

'Vera.' He continued holding his arm out and pointing at the door.

'First one day went by with no word. Then the second. On the third day I literally fell apart, Colin. Literally. I just started calling people. Anybody and everybody I could think of to ask if they'd heard anything.'

'Vera.'

'I reached a point where I was so frantic I didn't even know what I was doing. Calling people back I'd just called five minutes before. All hours of the night and day. By the time I was through the whole city was frantic. And I have to say, in Alicia's defence, once it sunk in to her the consequences of what we'd done she was just as desperate as I was.'

'That's touching, Vera, but please go now.'

'And when we found out you were all right . . . when Jeremy rang up and told us where you were – God, Colin, the relief. The two of us fell into each other's arms and wept for ten minutes. And you know what it would take to get Alicia and me to fall into each other's arms.'

'Could you hand me my trousers, Vera.'

'Your trousers.'

'On the arm of the chair.'

She removed them from the chair and carried them quickly over to him.

151

'Thank you,' he said, taking them. He stood up, loosening the towel around his waist and letting it fall to the carpet, then stepped into the trousers, pulling them up and buckling his belt.

'Where are your underpants.'

'Sorry?'

'It's none of my business, I just wondered why you didn't have any underpants on.'

'I was in a rush leaving the flat. Excuse me.' He walked past her and into the bathroom.

She followed him as far as the doorway, watching him take a shirt from a hook on the wall and put it on. 'Are you going out or something?'

'I might.'

'Well where.'

He went over to the sink, removed a comb from his back pocket and began combing his hair.

'I know you like to walk when you need to think. Is that what you're doing? Going for a walk so you can think?'

He glanced at her reflection in the mirror as he finished combing his hair. Then he returned the comb to his pocket. 'Excuse me, Vera.' He walked past her and into the next room, going to the corner where his shoes and socks were on the rug.

Vera didn't turn when he went past her but continued to stand where she was, looking into the bathroom and at a red portable hair dryer resting on the white porcelain lid on the tank of the toilet. Finally she walked over to it, studied it a few moments, then reached down to pick it up. 'Colin?' she called after holding it a few seconds. She looked over toward the door when he didn't answer, then walked to the open doorway just as Colin was removing his sketch pad and art supply case from the top of the bureau. 'Colin?'

'Yes.'

She held out the hair dryer.

'What do you want.'

'Does this belong to the motel?'

He looked at the object in her hand, then back at her. 'It's a hair dryer.'

'I know what it is, Colin. You don't use them, and I just wondered if the motel provides them for its guests.'

Colin walked across the room to the door and opened it.

'Colin.'

He stopped part way out the door. 'Yes?'

'Can't you just answer a simple question?'

He studied the hair dryer a few more moments. 'A simple one I could,' he said finally, 'but not that one.' He carried his sketch pad and case out past the Battlefield Inn sign, turned and started walking along the side of the highway.

10

When Colin got to Shining Shores it was lunchtime. He didn't go up to the front entrance, but walked across the gravel car park and around to the side of the main building, glancing in through a kitchen window where Mandy was transferring dirty dishes out of a cart and into a sink.

'Colin,' she said, looking over as he opened the door and stepped inside.

'Mandy.'

'I didn't expect you.'

He closed the door.

'Oh,' she said. 'You came to draw Mr West.'

'That's one thing.' He put his sketch pad and case on the table in the centre of the room. 'And there's something else.'

'What's that.'

He walked to her and took her hands, standing a moment and looking at her before speaking. 'The light on the telephone last night,' he said. 'It wasn't about paying.'

'What was it about.'

'Nothing's going to change between us, Mandy. I came out here right away, before doing anything else, to show you that nothing's going to be different now.'

'Colin, why are you being so dramatic.'

'Vera's here.'

She looked back at him without answering.

'In New Cardiff,' he said.

It was quiet for a few seconds as she continued to look at him.

Colin let go of her hands, reached into the cart and removed several dirty dishes from it to put in the sink. 'Keep working, Mandy. I don't want to give this event more importance than it deserves.'

'Vera's here?'

'She got in yesterday and came to the motel while we were out.'

'You've talked to her?'

'I've just come from talking to her.'

After a few more moments she turned and lifted some dirty silverware out of the cart to put in the sink.

'Now,' Colin said, setting two more plates in on the others.

'Well what did she say.'

'There'll be plenty of time to go into all that.'

'I mean I don't get it,' Mandy said. 'Is she here on her honeymoon or something?'

'There is no honeymoon.'

'Is her new husband with her?'

'There is no new husband,' Colin said. 'It was a phantom husband.'

'A what?'

'Mandy, I don't want to go into this now,' he said, putting the last of the plates in the sink. 'The point is, I came right here because you need to understand Vera's being here doesn't affect anything.'

'You don't have to keep saying that, Colin. I believe you.'

'She did a very unfortunate thing,' Colin said.

'What was that.'

'I don't want to discuss it now. I want to sketch Mr West, and go on normally.'

'Colin,' she said, 'you can't just come out here and put me in suspense like this and then not tell me why she's here. What was the unfortunate thing.'

'A joke.'

'A what?'

'She played a trick.'

'On who.'

'Myself.'

'She played a trick on you?'

'There was no wedding,' Colin said. 'There was no marriage. There was no Roger Pelham.'

Mandy frowned.

'Vera and her sister made it up.'

After a few more moments, Mandy looked down into the sink. 'I still don't . . .'

'They invented it.'

'Made it up? The wedding?'

Colin put some knives into the sink. 'I've more or less adjusted to it by now, after walking here and clearing my head. And I realise that Vera came all the way here because she feels very guilty, and she came all this way to try and clear her conscience.'

'Wait a minute,' Mandy said. 'It was all just made up? The whole wedding?

'I know, it's hard to—'

'The invitation,' she said.

'I guess they just had one printed up to send me.'

'One invitation printed up?'

Colin picked up a towel from beside the sink and dried off his hands.

'This is sick,' Mandy said.

'It was very upsetting to me at first,' Colin said, returning the towel to the shelf, 'and I didn't accept her apology. But now I've cooled down, and as soon as I do accept it I'm sure she'll turn around and go back to England.'

'You're going to accept her apology?'

'She needs absolution. Then she can go home.'

Mandy shook her head. 'I would never accept someone's apology if they did that to me.'

He put his hands on her shoulders. 'Okay. I came to draw Mr West.'

'I can't get over this.'

'For the moment, you'll have to.'

Mandy picked up the towel and dried her own hands. 'But how could anyone—'

'Mandy, think Mr West.'

She looked down at the linoleum floor. 'Mr West.'

'Is this a good time for me to do him?'

'Actually we have to do something before I take you to his room,' she said. 'I shouldn't really have gone ahead and arranged that.'

'Why not.'

'I mean it's going to be okay,' she said, going across the kitchen. 'I just should have gotten permission first.' She pushed open the door. 'We have to talk to Mrs Madison.'

'Who's that,' Colin said, walking out of the kitchen.

'The director.'

They went down a short hallway and into the dining room, where the residents were seated around a large table. Several of them looked up from their small plates of chocolate cake as Mandy led him through the room. Colin nodded at them, then followed her down another hall to a closed door. She stopped, waited a moment, then knocked.

A woman's voice came from the other side. 'Yes?'

'It's Mandy, Mrs Madison. My friend's here.'

'You may come in.'

Mandy opened the door. 'Go ahead, Colin.'

He walked into the room as a woman behind a desk rose and held out her hand.

'How do you do,' he said, shaking it.

'Mr Ware?'

'Colin Ware, yes.'

'How are you.'

'Fine. And very grateful for the opportunity to do the sketch.'

The woman sat down again.

'Shall I just take him down there?' Mandy said.

'Mr Ware, I'm sure you understand how it is, running a facility for older people. How careful we have to be that everything's done by the book.'

Colin nodded. 'I do.'

'Strictly speaking,' Mrs Madison said, 'I shouldn't be letting you do this.' She held up her hand to stop him from speaking. 'But you're a guest in our country, and that's why I'm going to bend the rules this time.'

'Well I don't want you to do it for that reason.'

'Now Mandy here is a great addition to Staff,' she said. 'All our residents are quite fond of her and she's a hard worker. But this is definitely not something she should have undertaken on her own authority.'

'Look,' Colin said.

'I did say I was sorry,' Mandy said.

Again Mrs Madison raised her hand for silence. 'As I mentioned before, you're a guest in our country, and I want you to take back nothing but pleasurable memories of your time here.'

'And I will,' Colin said, 'but I really don't want anyone to get in trouble over this.'

'May I ask how long you plan to be with us, Mr Ware?'

'In America?'

'Yes, in our country.'

'I'm not exactly sure.'

'You don't have a departure date.'

'Not yet.'

Again Mrs Madison rose from her chair and held out her hand. 'Are you enjoying your stay?'

'Very much,' he said, shaking it.

'And have you visited our monument yet?'

'Yes I have. Wonderful.'

'A momentous event occurred here, Mr Ware, in our nation's struggle for independence. The Battle of New Cardiff is greatly underrated in the history books, but it was one of the crucial turning points as we laboured to throw off the yoke of our cruel oppressor.'

'Very good,' Colin said, releasing her hand. 'Thank you.'

'And Mandy?' She looked over at Mandy, standing just inside the doorway. 'Stop by when you have a minute. I do need a word or two with you in private.'

'Yes, Mrs Madison.'

When Mandy showed Colin into Mr West's room, Mr West was asleep in a chair.

'He's asleep,' she said.

Colin nodded.

'We're not supposed to wake them up except for medication.'

'No.'

She gestured at the bed. 'You could sit there.'

Colin seated himself on the edge of the bed and looked back at Mr West. 'I didn't think someone could sleep sitting up that straight.'

'Can you do the drawing okay from there?'

'I think so.' He set his case on the bedspread and opened it, then laid several pencils out on the spread.

'I don't know what to tell you.'

'About what.'

'I mean I hope he wakes up,' she said, 'but I'm not sure he will right away.'

Colin looked at a collection of photographs in small frames on the bureau beside Mr West, then back at Mr West.

For a few seconds they watched him sleeping quietly in the chair.

'Would you want to have a picture of a sleeping person in your exhibit?'

'I might. I'd have to think about it.'

'Or how about this,' she said. 'You could go ahead and draw him like that, except for his eyes. Then draw his eyes when he wakes up. But Colin, I really can't stay.'

'No. You go, Mandy. We'll be fine.'

She stepped into the hallway and closed the door.

After she was gone, Colin sat looking at his subject a few moments longer, then he opened his sketch pad. He chose one of the pencils from the bedspread, held it over the page a few seconds as he studied Mr West's features, then began drawing his forehead.

Colin's concentration stayed mostly on the page, but one of the times he glanced up he saw that Mr West's eyes had come open and he was looking back at him. 'Oh,' Colin said. He set down the pencil. 'Yes.' Clearing his throat softly, he got up from the bed. 'Colin Ware,' he said, holding out his hand.

Mr West looked down at it but didn't extend his own.

'Mandy's friend.'

The man continued looking down at Colin's hand.

'Mandy the attendant,' Colin said. 'Short. Blond hair.'

Mr West slowly raised his hand and took Colin's.

'Yes,' Colin said, their two hands joined but remaining motionless. 'She mentioned you had very graciously agreed to sit for me.' He let go of Mr West's hand. 'And we also obtained the permission of Mrs Madison.' He returned to the bed, seated himself and picked up his pad. 'Why don't I just try to capture your very expressive eyes while we're talking here.' He began drawing one of Mr West's eyes but the second or third time he looked up both of them were closed again. He continued to work on the eye till it was finished. 'That's all right. I think I can . . . if need be I may be able to extrapolate from that one to the other.' He reached for the India rubber on the spread and rubbed out a line he'd made, but when he looked up again Mr West's head had tipped to the side. He sat a moment looking at it, then tilted his own head, glancing back and forth between Mr West and the page as he began drawing one of Mr West's ears. However, Mr West's head moved once again, this time forward, as his chin fell against his chest.

Colin sat several seconds looking at him, then got down off the bed and on to the floor, resting his pad on his legs and studying his face from below as he sketched.

It was fifteen or twenty minutes later, the drawing was nearly finished and Colin was working on the collar of Mr West's shirt, when suddenly Mr West twisted to the side, his head falling against his shoulder and his lips parting.

Colin's hand stopped on the page.

It was quiet in the room, except for the sound of a metal walker being moved slowly along the hallway on the other side of the door.

'Mandy!'

There was no answer.

After a few more moments Colin very carefully set his pad and pencil down on the carpet. Gradually he got to his feet.

Mr West remained perfectly still in the chair.

Colin glanced at the door, then looked back at his subject. He waited several more seconds, then began very slowly to move his hand toward the man's shoulder.

As Mr West lifted his head, opening his eyes, Colin lurched backwards, nearly falling.

'Yes,' he said, regaining his balance. 'Yes.' He bent down for his sketch pad. 'Mandy's friend.' He picked up his pencil and seated himself on the bed again. 'A great honour.' He glanced up at Mr West, then back down at the page, trying to draw for a second or two with the wrong end of the pencil before turning it around. 'Extremely gracious of you to sit.'

* * *

My always dearest Vera,

So many things are happening so quickly in both our lives right now that it's difficult to make complete – or any – sense of all the shifting planes of reality. However, as the mist clears, I can see that you followed me to America because, above all, you're a person of such high moral character that it was impossible to continue living with yourself after your thoughtless act.

Yes, Vera, you are fully and totally forgiven. One hundred per cent is your apology accepted. At first I dismissed Alicia's central role in this sorry saga, but I no longer do. She can be very crafty, and she has a mean streak that both of us have commented on. Without her influence, I'm sure you would have found a kinder way to tell me that the time has come for us to turn, each of us, to a new chapter in our lives, one where our friendship becomes stronger than it has been before, and where those 'romantic' elements, for want of a better word, are now set aside as we each look to new relationships to fill that dimension of our needs.

So as you now return home to England, please know that you carry all my love back with you – but a new and better kind of love, Vera. You carry back the kind of love that can only exist between two souls who have weathered so much together, and whose mutual understanding is so profound, that to try and continue with what one thinks of as a physical relationship would in fact cheapen that new plateau of affection between us that's been born out of this crisis.

It's unclear exactly when I'll be back in London, but the first thing we'll do when we arrive will be to ring you.

My love, and all thoughts are with you for a safe and relaxing journey home,

Colin

* * *

It was three days later that Colin called the Cardiff Arms Motel. 'I'm wondering if you could tell me if one of your guests has left,' he said.

'What's the guest's name.'

'Vera Edwards.'

It was quiet a few moments. 'She hasn't left,' the person said.

'She hasn't.'

'Shall I put you through?'

'No, no.' Again it was quiet. 'Is there any way to confirm if a letter was received by her recently.'

'Usually guests don't get mail here.'

'That's why I thought maybe someone might remember.'

'And you don't want to find out from her.'

'No.'

Again there was a pause.

'By any chance was this letter in an envelope from one of the other local motels?'

'It was.'

'Yes, I do recall giving her that.' The person on the other end waited several seconds, then said, 'Sir, either I'll have to put you through to her or discontinue this call.'

'Discontinue it.

1 1

There were two images in Mandy's mind by which she recognised Vera when she saw her in the car park outside the supermarket. The first came from a drawing Colin had brought with him from England. He hadn't told her about it, but in the bottom of his suit-case, several times Mandy had noticed a brown folder, and finally one night, as they were getting ready for bed, she had asked him what was in it. He'd said it wasn't anything important, just a draw-ing he'd done a few weeks before coming to America. When she asked if she could see it, he said it was up to her, then went into the bathroom and closed the door. She took it out of the folder and studied it for a long time. There was nothing on it to say who it was, but Mandy had no trouble figuring it out.

The other identifying image Mandy had in her mind wasn't of Vera herself, but of her car, which Joanie had described as a 'cute little blue Honda or something' when she was telling Mandy about Vera's first visit to the motel.

So on the afternoon Mandy was walking through the car park – an afternoon on which she'd been let out unexpectedly early from work, so that Colin hadn't been there to meet her – and she saw Vera unlocking the door of her car, she knew instantly who it was, and in fact stopped so suddenly when she recognised her that a woman behind Mandy accidentally rammed the wheel of her shopping trolley into Mandy's heel.

After the woman had pushed it around her, Mandy stood and watched as Vera set the bag containing her purchases over on to the passenger's seat of the car, then got in herself. Vera put her key into the ignition switch, turned on the engine, then pushed a button on the inside of the door, waiting as the window opened next to her.

As the glass sank down into the door, Vera became aware of the girl, standing a couple of parking spaces away, watching her. The two of them looked at each other a moment, then Vera reached up to pull her seat belt on before releasing the parking brake and glancing in the rear-view mirror.

'How could anyone do that.'

Vera turned her head to look back at the girl.

After speaking, she remained where she was, still looking intently at Vera. The only sound was the soft humming of Vera's motor.

'Were you talking to me?' Vera said finally.

'Yes.' The girl pushed some hair out of her face.

'I didn't hear what you said.'

'How could anyone do something that mean.'

Again it was quiet for several seconds.

'You know who I am?'

'Yes.'

'Who.'

'You're Vera.'

After another few moments, Vera reached down beside the steering column to turn off the engine. The two of them continued to study each other as an assistant from the supermarket walked between them.

'And may I ask your name?'

'Mandy.'

The assistant took hold of the handle at the end of a long row of trolleys and, leaning forward, pushed them slowly back between Vera and Mandy.

'Do you want to talk?' Vera said.

'We don't have to,' Mandy said. 'I just don't understand how someone could do what you did.'

Vera looked down at the top of her steering wheel for a few seconds, then back at Mandy. 'If we are going to talk,' she said, 'I'll get out.'

'It's up to you.'

Vera removed her seat belt, opened the car door again and got out. 'The mean thing,' she said, after closing the door. 'I assume you're referring to what I did to Colin Ware.'

'Yes.'

'Because to look out of the window when one's about to drive off with one's shopping,' Vera said, 'and be told by a stranger that they're mean, for some unspecified reason – that isn't what I think of as a formal introduction.'

'I should have said what I was talking about.'

Vera nodded. 'It was a cruel trick I played on him,' she said, 'wasn't it.'

'Yes.'

'We agree on that,' she said. 'Now I wonder if we could establish whether you have a red hair dryer.'

Mandy frowned.

'A little red portable one.'

'What does that have to do with anything.'

'Do you?'

'What if I do.'

'I'd never seen a bright red one before.'

Mandy shook her head.

'It wasn't yours?'

'I'm just saying what if it was. What if it was red. What if red happens to be my favourite colour. What does any of that have to do with you.'

Vera nodded. 'Now that we have been formally introduced,' she said, 'I will say that, yes, not only was it a very cruel thing to do to Colin – unprovoked and unprincipled – but beyond that I will add that it was thoroughly rotten, nasty and unforgivable.'

'He did forgive you,' Mandy said.

'What?'

'He forgave you for it already.' Mandy was standing on one of the painted lines that marked a parking space. A car moved slowly into the space just behind her and she took a step forward toward Vera.

'Colin's letter,' Vera said.

'He forgave you in that.'

'Did you read the letter Colin sent me?'

'He told me about it.'

A man got out of the car behind Mandy and walked toward the store.

'And I guess I can assume he told you about the part where he wished me a safe journey back to London.'

'Yes.'

'He told you that part.'

'Yes.'

'So in other words,' Vera said, making a gesture in Mandy's direction, 'that's what this is all about.'

'What.'

'Our little tête-à-tête,' she said, 'is about why I'm still here.'

Mandy shrugged.

'Is that not what it's about?'

'It's a free country,' Mandy said.

It was quiet for a moment. 'Help me understand the relevance of that observation.'

'You can do what you want,' Mandy said. 'But I would think after what happened, and the person did accept your apology, that you'd want to show them you really were sorry by letting them get on with their life.'

'On with their life.'

'If that's what they wanted to do.' Mandy shook her head slightly so hair no longer covered the side of one of her eyes.

'And I'm preventing Colin from getting on with his.'

Again Mandy shrugged.

Vera looked back at her a few moments in silence, then cleared her throat. 'This was the day I was giving up smoking, Mandy,' she said, 'but I just changed my mind.' She opened the car door and reached over to the glove box to take out a pack of cigarettes and a lighter. 'Do you smoke?' she said, coming back out and shutting the car door again.

'No.'

'Have you ever?'

'Yes.'

'When did you smoke.'

'In high school.'

Vera took a cigarette out of the pack and put it between her lips. 'And did you find it hard to give up?'

'Sort of.'

'Well I admire you.' She flicked the lighter and held the flame to the end of the cigarette till it was lit. 'Did you go to high school here?'

'Yes.'

'New Cardiff High? Something like that?'

'New Cardiff Regional.'

'Regional,' Vera said.

'Right.'

'And where's that,' Vera said. 'Nearby?'

'Over there,' Mandy said, pointing off past the supermarket. 'You can't see it from here.'

A four-by-four moved slowly between them and into a space. 'Why don't you come over here, Mandy. It seems a little chaotic to be conducting our discussion in the midst of moving traffic.'

Mandy walked across the two empty spaces that separated them.

'You seem like a nice person,' Vera said, as Mandy came to stand in front of her.

'Not really.'

'I'm sure you are,' Vera said. 'I'm sure Colin wouldn't spend time with someone who wasn't nice.'

'I'm sure you're nice too.'

Vera nodded. 'I'm sure all three of us are nice people.'

Mandy nodded.

'I do feel at a slight disadvantage, though,' Vera said, leaning back against the car, 'knowing nothing about you except the direction of your school and the colour of your hair dryer, while you probably know quite a bit more than that about me.'

'I don't know so much.'

'He hasn't told you much?'

She shook her head. 'We mostly talk about other things.'

Vera took a puff from her cigarette. 'I guess it would be private to ask what they were.'

'No,' Mandy said. 'Just the normal things people talk about.'

'The weather?' Vera said.

'We've talked about that.'

'What sort of day it is,' Vera said, 'that sort of thing.'

Mandy nodded.

'Whether it's cold or warm.'

'Right. Or windy.'

'Raining,' Vera said.

'Snowing,' Mandy said.

'Oh? Has it snowed here yet?'

'Not yet.'

'I see. You were planning one of your future conversations with him.'

Mandy watched her tap the ash from her cigarette. 'My point is we just talk about everyday things.'

'But he must have said some little thing about me since he's been here. You did know my name after all.'

'He's said things.'

'But those were just between the two of you.'

'No,' she said, 'he once mentioned you went to some islands together.'

'Islands.'

'I don't remember what they were called. I think they were down by Spain or somewhere.'

'The Canaries?'

Mandy nodded. 'Those were the ones.'

'How did that trip ten years ago come up.'

'He was trying to think of a peaceful place he'd been to and he thought of that.'

'A peaceful place.'

'Right.'

Vera looked down at the asphalt. 'It's nice to think of you and Colin sitting around remembering peaceful places you've been.'

'Look, you asked me what he'd said about you and that was one thing.'

'He probably didn't mention how we met.'

'How you met? Not really.'

'He didn't.'

'Not really,' Mandy said again. 'He did say you've known each other all your lives.'

'Actually longer than that,' Vera said. She took another puff on her cigarette. 'Although I can't imagine that this would be a particularly absorbing topic for you.'

'How could you know each other longer than all your lives.'

'He really didn't tell you this?' Vera said, turning her head so she wouldn't blow smoke in Mandy's face. 'It's by far his favourite story.'

'No.'

'I really am amazed.'

'How could you know each other longer than all your lives,' Mandy said again.

'Okay,' Vera said, 'since he didn't mention it – it is mildly amusing, I suppose, if you haven't heard it before. Anyway, our mothers had the same doctor. And they both happened to be in the doctor's waiting room one day at the same time, waiting for their appointments. They'd never seen each other before.'

'Your mothers.'

'Oh, they were pregnant,' Vera said. 'I almost left out the whole point of the story.'

Mandy nodded.

'So there they were, sitting side-by-side in two chairs. Are you absolutely sure Colin never . . .'

'He really didn't.'

'He would have, sooner or later. I don't think there's anyone else we know who hasn't heard the story from Colin at least a hundred times. So there they were, sitting in the two chairs, when one of us – and they've never been able to agree which one of us it was – kicked.' She took a quick puff from the cigarette. 'And that one's mother – you should hear the arguments, to this day, over which mother it was – put her hand on her tummy, turned to the other one beside her, and said, "Oh dear, that was a sharp one." Or words to that effect. At which point the other mother suddenly put her hand on her stomach and said, "There goes mine now. See what you've started." So that's how our mothers met, and I guess you could say that's how Colin and I met – it was a couple of months later that we came out, I was five days ahead of him – and of course the great family joke is that we've been kicking each other ever since.' Vera looked over at the supermarket and at an assistant carrying two heavy sacks of groceries out behind a customer. 'But this is honestly and truly the first time you've heard that story?' she said, looking back at Mandy.

'Yes.'

'Of course I'm so tired of it by now I go out of the room whenever it comes up,' Vera said, taking a final puff on her cigarette and dropping it beside her foot. She ground it out with the toe of her shoe. 'In July,' she said, 'when the two families were in Sweden, I said, "I am not leaving this hotel room till I have promises from every one of you that no one is going to make even the most oblique reference to The Story," – at this point it's just called The Story – but I actually made them swear not to bring it up before I'd go sightseeing with them.'

Mandy was looking down at the front tyre on Vera's car. 'The two families went to Sweden?'

'We all go on holiday together every July – the five of us, that includes Alicia, my little sister – it's one of God knows how many traditions that have sprung up between the two families over the years – Christmas, all the birthdays, so on and so on.' She glanced at Mandy, her head still bowed as she studied the ground. 'Of course whether any of the traditions survive Alicia's and my little wedding invitation caper remains to be seen. And on top of everything else – but you know about his father's situation.'

Mandy looked up at her. 'His what?'

'His father's health? I'm sure he mentioned that.'

'No.'

'Oh now, come on.'

'What about it.'

'Are you saying to me that Colin never even once mentioned his father's current health situation to you?'

'He hasn't.'

'Well this is just . . .' Vera shook her head. 'I'm flabbergasted.'

'Well could you tell me what it is?'

'Did he even tell you he has a family?' Vera said, frowning at her.

'Yes.'

'But nothing about them?'

'He told me about them.' She shrugged. 'He said they have a music store, they sell instruments and things.'

'The store,' Vera said, putting her hand up to her forehead. 'How will Iris cope with the business by herself if something goes wrong.'

'Vera, will you please tell me what's the matter with his father?'

'A few weeks ago, Colin Senior was diagnosed positive. So it's certain now he'll have to go in for the operation as soon as they can schedule him.'

'Diagnosed positive with what,' Mandy said.

Vera crossed her arms over her chest. She looked out toward the highway.

'Vera?'

'Mandy,' she said, keeping her face turned away, 'I'd prefer not to talk about this any more if that's all right. When I think of the consequences Alicia's and my thoughtlessness could have . . .'

'You don't have to talk about it,' Mandy said, 'but could you tell me one thing?'

'If I can.'

'The reason you're not going back to England,' Mandy said.

'Yes.'

'I mean the trick you played on Colin is why he came over here.'

Vera nodded.

'And you don't want to go back till he does.'

'True.'

'Okay, but how much of the reason you want him to go back is because of his father.'

'All of it.'

'All of it?'

'But I can't tell him that.'

'Why not.'

'I just can't, Mandy,' she said, shaking her head. 'I can see how much he enjoys being with you. It's such a nice change for him from all the doctors and hospitals, and the constant worry. I just don't have the heart to spoil the fun his trip to America turned out to be for him.'

'But why didn't he tell me about this.'

'He just didn't want to think about it for the time being. And I can understand that – can't you?'

'In a way maybe, but . . .'

A teenage boy wheeled a trolley piled high with cans of motor oil past them.

'I'd rather not talk about this any more,' Vera said.

'We don't have to, if it's painful.'

'Thank you.'

They glanced over at the boy as he bent down to pick up a can of oil that had fallen off.

'Anyway,' Vera said, 'there's a favour you could do for me if you wanted.'

'What's that.'

'But I don't want you to feel you have to.' She opened the door of her car again. 'It will probably seem a little unromantic,' she said, reaching across to her grocery bag on the far seat, 'so do say if you'd rather not.' She began rummaging around in the bag, then came back out of the car holding a cellophane-wrapped package in her hand. 'I could perfectly well drop these off at his room myself. I just thought if you were going over there anyway . . .' She held the package out to Mandy.

'Underpants,' Mandy said.

'But I really don't want you to be made to feel like an errand girl if it would take any of the fun out of things for you and Colin.'

'No, I can do it.' She took them from Vera.

'You're absolutely sure.'

'It won't take the fun out of things.'

'Because the other morning when I saw he'd gone off not even wearing underpants,' Vera said. 'Well let's just put it this way – I think it's in both our interests that the poor man doesn't have to go on walking around all day with the inside of his zip scraping against his private parts.'

Although Mandy nodded after Vera finished speaking, her gaze had returned to the general direction of the tyre.

Vera looked at her watch. 'I'm keeping you,' she said. She held out her hand. 'Mandy, I'm so glad we had the chance to meet and have our little talk. And I'm so reassured that Colin's in such good hands during this difficult time.'

Still without looking up, Mandy shook her hand.

'And maybe I don't seem quite the ogre you pictured either.'

'You don't.'

'Oh, good, Mandy.' Vera let go of her hand, got back in her car, pulled on her safety belt and drove away.

For a long time Mandy stood holding the underpants at her side, and looking at the empty space where Vera's car had been. Then someone whistled at her, and she turned and walked quickly to her own car.

When Colin got to Shining Shores he was told by one of her co-workers that Mandy had tried to call him when she found out she was leaving early, but when he hadn't been at the motel she told the co-worker to explain what had happened if Colin was there at five. She said she'd keep trying him during the afternoon, to save him an unnecessary trip, though obviously she had failed to make contact.

By the time Colin got back to the motel, she had been there and left.

As soon as he walked into his room he could tell by the empty hangers in the open closet that she'd gone.

He walked quickly to the closed door of the bathroom, pushed it open and looked inside. 'Mandy?'

He turned in a circle. 'Mandy.'

Colin hurried back across the room, and was about to go outside again when suddenly he stopped. He looked down at a cellophane-wrapped package on the seat of the chair and after a few moments reached down to pick it up. 'Vera.'

12

After she'd been in New Cardiff nearly a week Vera decided the time had come to resolve the issues between herself and Colin, and the place she chose for their discussion was a golf course she'd noticed on one of her drives around the town.

As she explained to Colin when she called to propose the meeting, the stresses she'd encountered in America, far from enabling her to give up her smoking habit – something she'd tried to do off and on over the years, and something she'd hoped the change of scene might help her accomplish – had caused it to escalate, and she was up to almost two packs a day, the highest consumption she'd ever attained.

Since there seemed nowhere indoors in New Cardiff to smoke, and since it wouldn't have been suitable for such a serious discussion simply to wander around the town smoking, she suggested the golf course, where she'd stopped the day before and learned it was permissible to smoke as long as a distance was kept from other golfers and the smoker carried the extinguished cigarette butts back to the clubhouse in a small plastic bag, which would be furnished prior to their going out on to the links.

With hundreds of accessible square miles in every direction, Colin asked, why did Vera not feel she could go off some place in the woods and smoke while they talked, but she responded that it was hard enough to concentrate in the rural village atmosphere of New Cardiff, but to be dwarfed by all of nature would altogether distract her from the matters at hand, and at least with a mown lawn under her feet, along with the pacifying effect of the nicotine, her anxiety might be reduced to levels where she could begin gaining perspective on the upheaval taking place in their lives.

Colin walked through the car park and toward the clubhouse, where Vera was standing beside the entrance. 'I've already paid our fees,' she said, as he approached. She held up a large plastic tag with '27' on it. 'This is our number.' She turned and started through the entrance.

'Vera?'

'It's too late to reserve a golf cart,' she said, looking back at him. 'I told them we probably wouldn't need a caddy.'

'Could you stop a minute?'

She stopped and came a step back toward him.

'Is all this supposed to be funny?' Colin said.

'What?'

'A caddy to carry your cigarettes around for you? Is that the gag? I want to be sure I'm not missing any classic humour here.'

'Colin, I always try to see the funny side of things – otherwise we'll end up jumping off a cliff. You taught me that.' She stepped aside while a man carrying a bag of clubs clicked past her in a pair of cleated shoes and went into the clubhouse.

'I got the impression we were meeting here for something serious.'

'We are.'

He nodded. 'You got my letter.'

'I did,' she said, 'and I was very touched.'

'Just not touched enough to do the right thing.'

She looked at him a moment before speaking. 'Colin, until certain questions are resolved I'm not just going to fly off into the sunset.'

Colin was about to say something more when he was interrupted by a loudspeaker on the wall of the clubhouse just above Vera's head. 'Will party twenty-seven report to the first fairway now.'

'That's us,' Vera said.

'Party twenty-seven to the first fairway now, please.'

Vera held a white card out to him.

'What's this.'

'Your scorecard.'

191

'I don't want a scorecard.'

'You have to have it.'

He took it, then followed her into the clubhouse and through a shop where clubs, caps, bags and other golf paraphernalia were displayed. 'By the way,' Vera said, 'did you get the underpants?'

He passed a sweater that had been shaped so that its arms appeared to be drawn back as if ready to swing a club.

'Colin?'

'Ask me again, Vera. A little louder this time. I don't think they quite heard you out on the number eight hole.'

'Are you party twenty-seven?' a woman said, as Vera came to her desk.

'Yes.'

'You need to get right out there.'

'Sorry.'

'Did you want to rent golf shoes, sir?' the woman said to Colin, glancing at his shoes as he followed.

'No.'

'Where are your clubs.'

'Already out there.'

Party twenty-eight, two women in short white pleated skirts, was sitting on a bench at the first tee. Vera walked out of the clubhouse and toward them. 'I hope you weren't waiting for us.'

'Twenty-seven?' one of the women said.

Vera showed them her numbered tag. 'But go ahead. We'll wait for you to go first.'

'You have to go in order,' the other one said.

Vera looked back at Colin as he caught up. 'We have to go in order.'

'I heard.'

'We'll go quickly,' Vera said to the women.

The two of them turned their heads to watch Colin as he passed them. 'Hi,' he said. They didn't answer.

Vera had started across the large grassy area stretching down from the tee.

'Vera?' he said, coming after her.

She held out a short yellow pencil to him.

He shook his head.

'Just take it, Colin.'

'I will not.'

They walked side-by-side in silence for a while, till finally Colin turned his head to look back at the two ladies.

'Are they starting yet?' Vera said.

'One of them's putting her ball down on the tee.'

He continued walking with his head turned back so he could keep his eye on the ladies. 'Will you please light up so we can get this over with?' he said.

'What are they doing now.'

When she had finished placing her ball on the tee, the woman held the club up over her head in both hands, turned one way, bent backwards and then turned the other way and lifted up her knee.

'Colin?'

'She's exercising.'

'Tell me when she's going to hit it.'

'No. You might get out of the way.'

Tripping slightly as he looked back, Colin watched the woman step away from the tee and take a swing.

'Now what's she doing.'

'Can't you look for yourself?'

'Tell me.'

'Practising her swing.'

Vera looked down at her scorecard, turning it over as she walked. 'There's a map of the golf course on the back of these.'

'I wasn't too worried about getting lost. Okay, she's about to hit it.'

Vera ducked.

'She's hitting it from back there, Vera. Good God.'

The woman took two little steps up and down, then drew back her club, hesitated a moment and swung. There was a click.

'Where is it.'

'In the air.'

'Where in the air.'

'Just in the air, Vera.'

'Coming toward us?'

'Going toward some trees.'

'Tell me when it lands.'

'It just did.'

'Where.'

'Not on your head,' he said. 'What else matters.'

'Where did it land.'

He pointed over toward a thicket of trees as they walked.

'I don't see it.'

'Open your eyes.'

'Oh it's yellow. I was looking for white.'

Colin lowered his arm, glancing behind as the second woman bent over to set her ball on the tee. 'Is this what you meant by a thoughtful and wide-ranging discussion by two mature adults to sort out the course of their future lives?'

'I'm ready to start,' Vera said, keeping several paces ahead of him.

'Then do.'

'All right,' she said. 'First of all, I'm sure your friend mentioned the little chat we had in the car park the other day.'

'My friend has a name, Vera.'

'Mandy,' she said. 'Sorry.'

Behind them was a click.

'Where's that one going.'

'Same place.'

'Tell me when it lands.'

They walked a few seconds in silence.

'It has.'

'What I'd like to say about Mandy,' Vera said, 'is that she's a very sweet person.'

Colin caught up with her.

'I can't imagine anyone not liking her,' Vera said. 'She's just very vivacious and bubbly and fun.'

They walked a few more moments in silence.

'Vera?'

'Yes, Colin.'

'I'm stupefied.'

'Why are you stupefied.'

'What a wonderful list of adjectives for Mandy.'

'I'm just telling you how she struck me.'

'Shouldn't you be writing them all down on your scorecard?' He walked a little faster to keep up with her. 'But Vera,' he said, 'surely among all the superlatives there must have been one negative.'

'I didn't notice any.' She opened her bag as they walked.

'These are qualities I haven't even discovered in Mandy myself.'

'I'm sure you will,' she said, looking through the bag.

'And they all just came gushing out there by the supermarket? It must have drawn a crowd.'

Gradually Vera came to a stop, but continued to rummage through her bag.

Colin stopped beside her.

'Shit,' she said finally.

'I don't believe it.'

'Wait here,' she said, closing the bag.

'I won't.'

'While I run and get them.'

'No.'

'You won't wait here for three minutes?'

'So you can come back and start telling me more lies?'

'What lies are these now.'

'About your feelings, Vera. Just say you didn't find Mandy very bright. Is that so hard?'

'Colin, however bright I may or may not have found Mandy, it doesn't mean she isn't sweet and fun, which are the qualities that make her such a welcome distraction for you at the moment.'

'Fore!'

They turned to see the two women standing by the trees.

'Fore!' one of them called again.

'Is she talking to us?' Vera said.

'I believe so.'

The woman drew back her club and swung. Colin and Vera looked up as the ball sailed over their heads, finally falling next to a sand trap.

'Will you walk with me back to the car park then.'

'No.'

'Because I really do need a cigarette, Colin, if you're going to extol Mandy's intelligence.'

'Is that what I was going to do?'

'You were warming up to it.'

The second woman drew back her club and swung. There was a click, and they looked up to see her yellow ball sail over their heads.

'Where'd that one go.'

'In the sand,' Colin said.

Vera looked ahead at the next tee, where two men were standing beside a golf cart. She bent forward slightly and squinted toward them. 'Is that person smoking?' she said. 'The one in the orange sweater.'

'I have no idea.'

'He is.' She started toward them.

Colin glanced at the two women, who looked silently back at him as they pulled their bags in his direction.

'Nice shot,' he said. He watched them go past, then hurried after Vera. 'They hate us,' he said as he reached her.

'Maybe that kindred spirit up ahead will put me out of my misery.'

He walked quietly beside her. 'I don't appreciate being put in a position where people hate me, Vera.'

'No one hates you.'

'Those ladies do. You didn't see the looks.'

'Well who cares if they do.'

'I care.'

'Why.'

'Because I'm a person of love and understanding.'

Ahead of them one of the men was loading his bag of clubs into the back of the cart as the other climbed into the small vehicle.

'Excuse me,' Vera said, hurrying toward them.

They stopped, turning to look at her.

'I'm terribly sorry to bother you like this,' she said, 'but I noticed you smoking as we were approaching, and I stupidly left my own cigarettes in the car. Is there any chance I could trouble you for one?'

Stepping back out of the cart, the man reached in through the V-neck of his sweater to remove a pack of cigarettes from his shirt pocket. 'British?'

'Yes we are,' she said, glancing at Colin. 'Yes.'

He shook the pack so that several of the cigarettes came partially out of it. 'What brings you our way.'

'Thank you so much,' Vera said, taking one.

'Take several.'

'Really?'

'Help yourself.'

She took two more.

The man shook the pack so that several more stuck up out of it, and held it in Colin's direction.

'I don't. Thank you.'

'What brings you our way,' he said again, returning the pack to his pocket.

'The foliage,' Colin said.

'I left my lighter in the car too.'

The man reached into his pants pocket for a pack of matches. 'Those are yours,' he said, handing them to her.

'This is so very nice of you.'

'Where are your clubs,' the other man called over from the cart.

'We're just getting a feel for the layout of the course first,' Colin said.

'Have a good one,' the man in the sweater said, getting back into the cart.

Colin held up his arm, waving as they drove off.

The first match went out but Vera cupped her hands around the second one long enough for her to puff on the cigarette till it was lit. She took a deep drag and closed her eyes, holding the smoke in her lungs for several seconds before slowly exhaling it.

'Vera?'

'Yes, Colin.'

'Not to spoil the magic,' he said, 'but since the reason for the cigarette was so you could stand hearing something about Mandy besides that she's bubbly and fun, I might say a word or two in her defence now.'

'I want you to.'

'You don't, but I will anyway.'

'Colin, I want to learn to like Mandy.'

'And as for the patronising remarks,' he said, raising his scorecard, 'one more and I'll use the map on this to find my way out of here.'

She held out her cigarette and tapped it to knock off a couple of flicks of ash. 'Touchy.'

'Mandy leads me to subjects,' he said.

'She what?'

'She's able to find subjects for me to draw. No one's ever done that before.'

Vera took a second drag, not as deep as the first. 'I thought you liked to find your own subjects.'

'But she finds them anyway. She put me together with her brother. Then a chemist. And an elderly man at the home where she works. He could barely stay alive for his portrait, but it still turned out.'

'I'm sure I could find subjects for you,' Vera said, 'if I thought that's what you wanted.'

He shook his head.

'At least let me try, Colin, if that's one of her attractions for you.'

'You couldn't.'

'I could learn to.'

'Maybe Mandy and I think alike visually. If there is such a thing.'

'You and I think alike, Colin.'

Again he shook his head.

She took another puff. 'We always have.'

'Not really. And the only way you could ever think like Mandy, Vera, would be to unlearn things. And that's not something you can do.'

'Unlearn what.'

'I don't know. Maybe everything.'

'Would a lobotomy be a good place for me to start?'

'You'd have to unlearn how to say things like that.'

Vera looked down at a lump of earth that had been turned over near her foot. 'Odd,' she said, 'I thought that sounded like something you'd say.'

'And it is,' he said. 'And that's my point. If we do think alike it's in the wrong way. We don't even know where one of us ends and the other begins any more. But it's time for us to break into two parts now. And each part move off in its own direction. And face it, Vera, even you have to admit your little wedding prank had the purpose of ending things between us. Consciously or not.'

With the toe of her shoe Vera turned the piece of turf back over to cover the bare spot. 'No. I'll admit that was the most awful thing I've ever done. And how I could have done it to you will always be beyond me. But if I did it to end things, why did I come over here.'

'Because of how guilty you felt, but that doesn't change the reason you did it.' He watched her walk slowly to another piece of over-turned sod. 'Every friend we've ever had has told us at one time or another, they're mystified at why we've stayed together so long.'

'What friend told us that.'

'What friend didn't.'

'We've had this argument so many times before.'

'We endlessly have it.'

She turned the second piece of turf right-side-up with her toe. 'I can even tell you the next thing you're going to say.'

'You keep making my point for me, Vera.'

'That you've huddled in my shadow all these years because I have all the social poise and you lack confidence with other people.'

He nodded.

'Weren't you going to say that.'

Colin walked over to where Vera had been standing before. 'It was in the queue.'

'And that half the time you feel like just another of Vera's Treasures, whatever you mean by that.'

With his shoe he turned the first tuft of grass back over to expose the dirt again.

'And you'll end up by saying the main reason we've stayed together so long is only because our families are such close friends we don't want to rupture their relationship.'

Colin looked over at the women. One was standing in the sand trap. She hit her ball up on to the green.

'But haven't we had enough angst for a while, Colin? Would you mind if I tried to lighten the mood a bit?'

'Be my guest.'

'I've wanted to tell you this thought I had yesterday,' she said, again tapping the ash off her cigarette. 'Let me think where I was. Oh. I was sitting in the McDonald's on Main Street.'

'By any chance is this some profound insight into American culture we're about to hear.'

'How'd you know that.'

'Just say it, Vera.'

'That's uncanny. How did you know that.'

'That's how Siamese twins work.'

'Incredible,' she said. 'But I was sitting there reading the paper. And I looked up and I thought, "Vera? Here you are in America, where freedom of speech is revered more highly than anywhere else in the world . . ."'

'Vera.'

'Can I finish?'

'Whenever you start referring to yourself in the third person there's trouble looming.'

'I won't do that.'

'Thank you.'

'Anyway, it was the second person.' She took another puff. 'But I looked up from the paper. And it hit me. Isn't it odd, I thought, that the country with the most freedom of speech has the people in it with the least to say.'

Colin had turned back toward the women. One was on the green, standing over her ball. She drew her club back a few times, then putted the ball toward the hole.

'Isn't that ironic?'

'Can we go back now.'

'You don't want to compare our impressions of America.'

The woman walked across the green, bent down and removed her ball from the hole.

'No.'

'Then could I ask one last question about Mandy?'

'One.'

'Did I hear you say she works in a home?'

'I said it. It would appear you heard me.'

'Administrative work or something?'

The women had finished the first hole. They walked to their golf bags, pushed their putting irons down into them, then wheeled the bags away from the green.

'I'm in the early stages of an extremely severe Vera headache,' Colin said.

'Can't you tell me what she does at the home?'

'Washes people.'

'Really?'

'Among other things.'

'Like what.'

'She feeds them, Vera. She turns them over.'

Vera nodded. 'I can see Mandy being very good at turning people over.'

He started walking away. 'Bye.'

'Colin, I'm sorry I said that. Mandy's a very kind person to do that sort of work. I'm not a kind person. You've gone to her because you need someone who's kind right now, and it's very painful for me. But I shouldn't have said that.'

He stopped but didn't look back at her.

'And I know she's waiting for you. But I wish you'd give me just a couple more minutes.'

'She's not waiting for me.'

'No?'

'After making her underwear delivery the other day,' he said, turning back toward her, 'she left.'

'Really.'

'Yes really, Vera.'

'Well I'm sure you see her.'

'Actually I don't,' he said. 'I've gone twice to her work, but each time her co-worker has come out to tell me how busy she happens to be at that particular moment.'

Vera looked over at the women who were speaking to each other and looking back at her as they pulled their golf carts over the grass in their direction. 'Well I really don't think it was my fault she moved out, Colin. I was utterly polite to her in the car park.'

'I'm sure.'

Vera took a final drag on the cigarette. 'I was,' she said. 'Ask her.'

'How. She's gone.'

After she'd exhaled, Vera bent down to lift up the piece of sod she'd turned over before, dropped the cigarette and replaced the divot over it.

'May we conclude our little forum now with our mission statements,' Colin said.

'Go ahead.'

'Neither of us knows how to say goodbye, Vera. We both want to. We're miserable, clinging to each other because we don't know how to do anything else, but each of us desperately wishes we could think of some way out of the relationship without bringing our worlds crashing down around us.'

'No, Colin,' she said, glancing at the approaching women. 'I made a very serious mistake. I'm now getting what I deserve. And when you feel I've been punished enough, we'll get in my hired car, drive it down to New York together, drop it off at the airport, fly home and this unhappy chapter will be over.'

The two women pulled their bags up on to the tee area and stopped several yards from Colin and Vera. They all stood looking at each other for a few seconds, then one of the women turned her eyes down to a wisp of smoke rising up from under the piece of sod beside Vera's foot. 'What's that.' she said.

'Smoke,' Colin said.

'You're allowed to smoke as long as it doesn't bother other people,' Vera said. 'I should have picked up a little plastic bag to carry the cigarette butt back in, but unfortunately I forgot.'

One of the women glanced at her partner. 'You may be able to smoke on the course,' she said, looking back at Vera, 'but you didn't read the other rules in there very closely.'

'Actually I did,' Vera said.

'The rules on the clubhouse wall,' the second woman said.

Vera nodded. 'I read them.'

'Which rule or rules do you feel we're not obeying,' Colin said.

'The rule to play golf,' one of them said, turning toward him.

The other one looked at Vera. 'The rule that when you're on a golf course you play golf.'

'Which one was that,' Vera said.

'What?'

'Which number rule was that.'

'Number?'

'Oh a comedienne,' her partner said. 'We've got a comedienne.'

'I'm not trying to be funny,' Vera said. 'You asked if I'd read the rules. I said I had. Then he asked you which rule we were breaking.'

'Excuse me, Vera,' Colin said, stepping forward. 'Maybe I can . . .' He nodded, then turned to one of the women. 'My friend and I needed a chance to have a private talk together.' He paused a moment, then faced the other woman. 'And as it happens, she's trying to give up smoking at the moment.'

'Sir.'

'May I just quickly explain,' Colin said.

'I know what to say,' Vera said, stepping forward.

'Miss?' said the woman standing a foot or two behind her partner. 'Are you playing golf?'

'Am I?'

'A very simple question, miss. Are the two of you playing golf or are the two of you not playing golf?'

'We're not.'

'Well we are, miss.'

'I know.'

'Because it's a golf course,' she said, 'and guess what people do on golf courses.'

'I think I've just put my finger on the basis of the misunderstanding here,' Colin said.

'Sir, answer my friend's question please.'

'What was it.'

'What do people do on golf courses.'

'For the most part they play golf.'

'Bravo, sir.'

For a long time it was quiet as the four of them stood looking at each other, then finally Colin cleared his throat softly and turned to the woman nearer him. 'My friend and I have some fairly deep-seated personal problems that go back to our childhoods.'

Vera had started back toward the clubhouse. 'Colin?'

'And quite by chance,' Colin said to the women, 'we find our-
selves here on this beautiful golf course as we try to work through
these difficult issues.'

'Colin.'

'But you're right,' he said, taking a step back, 'this is not the place
to try and come to grips with private matters. So let me apologise . . .'

'Colin!'

'. . . if our personal difficulties have impacted negatively on your
enjoyment of the number one hole. And in our absence I'm sure
your enjoyment of the number two hole will proceed as it should.'
He turned around and hurried after Vera.

13

It had become Colin's habit to go across the street each morning for breakfast at the Deep Cup Diner, and it was on one of these trips that Joanie called to him as he approached the highway. She was standing next to the maids' room. 'Colin?' She motioned for him to come. 'Could I see you a minute?'

She finished giving instructions to a maid as Colin walked toward her, then came to meet him in front of one of the rooms.

'I haven't seen much of you lately,' she said. 'What's going on.'

'Not much.'

The door beside them opened and a man came out with his

suitcase. 'Let's just step out of the way here.' She took his sleeve and led him off a few feet. 'What have you been doing.'

'This and that,' Colin said. 'Reading.'

'Oh?' she said. 'In your room?'

'No, actually at the library.'

'Don't you just love our little library?' she said. 'Listen, I can't really talk now, but Mandy called.'

'She did?'

'Last night,' Joanie said, reaching into her shirt pocket for a piece of paper. 'She wanted me to give you this.'

Colin took it.

The man had put his suitcase into the boot of his car, which was backed up to his room, and was holding out his plastic entry key. 'What do we do with these.'

'Just leave it in your room,' Joanie said, smiling at him. 'Did you have a nice night, sir?'

'It was okay.'

'I'm so glad.'

He returned inside.

Colin was studying the slip of paper she had given him. 'Who's Doug Reed,' he said.

'That's his phone number,' she said, pointing at a number on the paper. 'And this is his address over at the Chamber of Commerce.'

'But who is he.'

'Okay, Doug's an all-round great guy. We recruited him out of Hartford a couple years ago to give our town a little more pizzazz. Which he's done like a house afire – our tourist trade is way up. You'll fall in love with Doug just like the rest of us have.'

'And his name came from Mandy.'

'That's right.'

'She thought I needed a friend? I don't . . .'

'No, no, Colin, he was out at the Shores for some reason yesterday, he and Mandy were chatting, and I guess it came up that he'd be happy to sit for his portrait, if you'd be interested.'

'Oh,' Colin said, 'oh.'

'Unless you have all the drawings you need.'

'No, I don't.' Colin folded the slip of paper, removed his wallet and put it in with his dollar bills. 'Well thank you so much, Joanie.'

'Don't thank me, Colin,' she said. 'You know who to thank.'

He returned the wallet to his back pocket.

'Colin?'

'I do,' he said, 'and I will.'

Beside them the man's wife came out of the room with a clothes bag and set it into the open boot on top of the suitcase.

'It was hard, wasn't it,' Joanie said, 'for her to keep staying here once her job started again. She needed that structure of her apartment, didn't she, when she went back to work.'

'If she calls again,' Colin said, 'I hope you'll put her through.'

'I told her last night I was sure you'd want to talk to her.'

'Of course I did.'

'But she said it was late and she didn't think she should bother you.'

'What time was it.'

'Seven-thirty.'

The man came out to open the door of his car, reached inside to turn on his engine, then went back into his room again.

'I wish people wouldn't warm their cars up like that,' Joanie said, waving her hand in front of her face, 'they stink up the whole place. Come down here.' She walked off in front of the next room and Colin followed. 'She is in the phone book, you know, Colin. I think there's just one M Martin in there. There's no law against calling people up.'

'I went to Shining Shores twice, Joanie.'

'And.'

'She doesn't want to see me at the moment.'

'Well call her, Colin. She's out there working away for God's sake. Call her up at home when she can talk.' Joanie shook her head. 'Don't be such a mouse.'

'I'm not being a mouse, Joanie.'

'Of course you are.'

'Joanie, sometimes there's a fine line between a mouse and a stalker.'

'Colin,' she said, 'that is by far the most ridiculous thing I've ever heard anyone say in my entire life.'

The door beside them opened and a woman came out carrying a pillow. Colin watched her walk across the car park with it. 'Is she stealing that?'

'Some guests like to bring their own.'

'Oh.'

They watched her put it into her car.

'She misses you, Colin.'

'Did she say that?'

'She didn't have to.'

'Look, I have to get some breakfast.' He started away.

'Is Vera still in town?'

He stopped. 'Yes.'

'Where's she staying.'

'The Cardiff Arms.'

'Oh they're very good. They won the Hospitality Award three years ago, the year we missed because Fisher's back was out.' It was quiet a moment. 'What are her plans.'

'Vera's?'

'Does she have any?'

Colin shrugged. 'She doesn't seem to have that many.'

'Just enjoying our little corner of the world for a while I guess,' Joanie said.

'That's a good way to put it.'

Again it was quiet, except for traffic passing on the highway.

'Call Mandy, Colin.'

'I want to.'

'Don't "want to",' she said, 'pick up the phone and do it.'

'I will.'

'Promise me?'

'Yes.'

'Say it.'

'I promise I'll call Mandy.'

'Enjoy your breakfast,' she called after him, as he hurried across the highway.

When Colin got to the Chamber of Commerce, Doug was standing beside his desk talking on the phone with someone about installing a historical marker next to the covered bridge. 'They shouldn't have to get out of their car to read it,' he said, as Colin stopped outside the open doorway. 'Big lettering. Not more than two or three short sentences. Keep it simple, Brad.' He motioned for Colin to come into the office. 'Here's a thought. Why don't you put together a mock-up of the thing there at your plant and I'll come over and drive past it in my car. We'll figure out how much a person can grab with their eyes at twenty miles an hour or whatever the bridge speed limit is.' As Colin entered the office, Doug pointed at a chair on the other side of his desk. Colin seated himself, resting his case and drawing pad in his lap. 'What should it say? Brad, you keep asking me that. For the mock-up just put "Mary had a little lamb" or something on it.' Doug leaned across the desk briefly to shake Colin's hand. 'You're a broken record on this final version thing, Brad. We'll cross that bridge later – forgive the pun. But show me one covered bridge in this state that doesn't have a historical marker next to it. Just one. You can't. Except ours. And that's a disgrace, Brad. It reflects on us all. Get that mock-up ready by Wednesday.' He hung up the phone. 'Colin Ware, the British artist,' he said, seating himself and grinning across the desk at Colin. 'Mandy out at the Shores tells me I'm going to be immortalised today.'

'I'll do my best.'

'Oh listen, before we get started,' he said, pointing to a water cooler in the corner, 'have you sampled our spring water yet.'

'I haven't.'

He got up again. 'It's in all the local stores as of last month,' he said, walking across the room. 'And if you're wondering what makes ours so special, it's because it comes from deeper in the earth than any of your more well-known waters.' He removed two paper cups from a holder on the wall. 'So it's older. Now you might not think you want older water.'

Colin watched him fill one cup from the cooler, then the other. 'But it sounds like maybe I do.'

'Old is good, so says my geologist,' Doug said, carrying them back across the room. 'It sits down there and ages, like wine, then has farther to travel up to the top, more sedimentation to go through, which means more purification.' He handed Colin a cup and carried the other around his desk and sat down again.

It was quiet for a moment as the two of them drank the water.

'What do you think,' Doug said.

Colin nodded. 'A nice fresh taste.'

'You like it.'

'And old,' Colin said. 'A nice fresh old taste.' He finished his water.

'By this time next year, we'll be crowding your other New England waters off the shelf.' Doug finished his and dropped the cup into a wastebasket beside the desk. 'My geologist refers to New Cardiff Deep Spring Water as the sleeping giant of the twenty-first century.' He reached across for Colin's cup. 'And as soon as I come up with the right gimmick,' he said, dropping it into the basket too, 'waters of America? Watch out. You've been given fair warning.' He looked down at the computer keyboard in front of him. 'Colin. Would you mind if I just quickly went through this little dah-dah-dah I do with foreign visitors.'

'My pleasure.'

'Won't take a minute.' He tapped a key to light up the monitor screen beside him. Colin watched as he tapped several more, then put his hands over the keyboard. 'How are we spelling that last name today, Colin. W-a-r-e? Or W-e-a-r.'

'The former.'

He typed it. 'Nationality, British. Good old John Bull.' He glanced up at Colin. 'Hometown? Don't tell me. London.'

'Correct.'

'Had to be, had to be, man of the world that you obviously are.' He typed it in. 'Okay. Reason for coming to New Cardiff.'

He held his hands over the keyboard waiting for Colin to answer, then looked up at him again when he didn't.

'Art,' Colin said.

'Could we be a little more specific.'

'I'm preparing an exhibition.'

'More specific still?'

'I'm doing drawings of some of the people here – such as the one of yourself – for an exhibition in London in the spring.'

'That's what I need.' He typed it in. 'What's the title of your show.'

'I don't give them titles.'

'Always a first time.' Doug looked up over Colin's head for a few seconds. 'Here's one for you. "Faces of New Cardiff, Vermont – Birthplace of American Art."'

'Birthplace?' Colin said.

'Does that have a ring to it?'

'How is New Cardiff the birthplace of American art.'

221

'Don't get testy, Colin, I'm just trying to help. By the way, have you ever been to the other one? It's over there by you.'

'Other what.'

'Cardiff,' Doug said. 'The old one.'

'Oh. Yes I have.'

'What's that one like.'

'Yes,' Colin said, nodding, 'I can easily see how the original settlers might compare this landscape—'

'Let's talk settlers later,' Doug said, typing again. 'First we need to finish up this little dah-dah-dah. Now. I want you to be totally frank with me, Colin, that's the only way we grow, people like yourself being honest about how they see us. "Doug," they said when they hired me, "you're here to suck those tourist bucks into New Cardiff, don't let them keep floating over to Bennington or Brattleboro any more." So lay it on me, friend. How can we improve on our little piece of heaven.' He stopped talking, fingers remaining on the keyboard as he looked over at Colin, waiting for him to answer. 'Don't spare my feelings. That's not how New Cardiff grows.'

'How to improve the town,' Colin said.

'Big things. Small things. Whatever comes to mind.'

Colin looked down at a corner of the desk.

'I can take it,' Doug said.

'I'm not hesitating because I don't think you can take it.'

'Hit us with your best shot.'

'It's a beautiful little town,' Colin said. 'Clean. Very friendly people.'

'But,' Doug said.

'What?'

'I'm waiting for that "but" to come winging across the table.'

'No buts,' Colin said, 'although there is one thing I've noticed.'

'I'll settle for an although.'

'I don't know if this is exactly a criticism,' Colin said, 'it's more of a question. But it seems every time I go out I see a shopping centre I didn't notice before. Almost like they spring up overnight while I'm sleeping. And I can't help but wonder how this tiny little village supports them all.'

'Commerce,' Doug said, typing. 'Good subject, good subject. Have you shopped Main Street yet.'

'Yes.'

'And how have you found our merchants generally.' But suddenly, before Colin could answer, Doug looked up and began grinning at him across the desk. 'You're an artist,' he said.

Colin nodded.

'And you've shopped Main Street.'

'Yes.'

After another few moments Doug crossed the fingers on both his hands and looked up at the ceiling. 'Dear God, please make this happen. Please, oh please, make this the happiest day of my life.'

He looked back down at Colin. 'Don't answer this question yet,' he said, getting up. 'I'm going to ask it but I don't want you to answer it till I tell you to.' He went to a filing cabinet and pulled open one of its drawers. 'Have you shopped Petersons Art Supply. Don't answer.' He removed a folder bulging with papers from the drawer and returned with it to his seat. 'Just answer this much,' he said. 'Do you know where Petersons is, are you familiar with it.'

'The little shop selling artists' materials?'

'You know the store I'm talking about.'

'Yes.'

Doug set the folder down beside the keyboard of his computer, then put his hands together in a praying position and again looked up at the ceiling. 'Dear God,' he said, 'make this be true. Make my prayers for the last year-and-a-half come true on this day. Just let Colin Ware be a person who has shopped Petersons and I'll know that we live in an intelligent universe.'

Frowning slightly, Colin watched him from his side of the desk.

'Well?' Doug said.

It was quiet.

'Well?' he said again.

'Me or God.'

'You.'

'Have I shopped at Petersons Art Store?'

Doug closed his eyes, his face tipped upwards, his hands still together.

'I have,' Colin said.

'Have what,' Doug said, eyes tightly shut. 'I need to hear the words.'

'Shopped there.'

'Shopped where.'

'Petersons Art Store. It was the first thing I did here.'

Doug raised his arms up toward the ceiling. 'The first thing! Yes!' He jabbed his fist at the air. 'Shopping Petersons was the first thing he did here! Yes! Yes!'

'Although I'm not sure it merits this much excitement.'

Doug brought his chair up closer to the desk. 'I have here the Petersons horror stories file,' he said, opening the folder. 'I won't go into all the cases. Suffice it to say, of the many fine artists that live in our community, not one of them – and I do mean not one single local artist – will set foot in there. A two-hour drive up to Rutland and back for a tube of paint is preferable to the chronic depression following a purchase from Martha or Harold Peterson.' He removed one of the sheets of paper from the folder. 'Let's pick a random sample,' he said, looking at it. 'Good. Definitely top ten stuff. Top five. Maybe even my all time number one.' He held up the form. 'A very fine Nigerian gentleman. A water colourist. Visiting from his homeland, wearing the costume of his nation, the robes and whatnot, very stately, one of his country's finer artists as it turned out, here to render some New England scenery. By the way, if you're wondering how two Neanderthals happen to be running an art shop, I'll give you a quick fill-in.' He leaned back in his chair. 'Daughter Judy had it first. A highly competent part-time artist herself, daughter Judy had built up a thriving little business, when mom and dad, recently out of the heating-oil business, decided retirement was getting a little stale and wouldn't it be fun to help Judy out over at the store. How different can it be selling yellow ochre than it was flogging number ten grade diesel oil, right? Long story short – it's now a mom and pop operation, and last I heard Judy was in an institution for the incurably insane up in Montpelier.' Doug frowned. 'Where was I – I've lost my thread.'

'The Nigerian artist.'

'Right. Timbu.' He nodded. 'So. Needing a new brush, he takes a stroll from his motel over to Petersons to pick one up.' Doug put Timbu's form back with the others. 'But he never gets inside. He never even gets to the front door. When they see him coming – his robes, headgear – Martha runs up and locks it while Harold calls the police to say there's a terrorist approaching the establishment. Out comes the shotgun from under the counter, and our gentle visitor is left to contemplate an obese American holding up a firearm and glaring at him through the glass till a squad car squeals around the corner.' Doug closed the folder. 'Now I know you can't match that one, and I'm not asking you to. It's my *pièce de resistance*, and you shouldn't feel badly that you can't rise to that level. But last council meeting, Colin, I came this close . . .' He put his thumb and forefinger almost together. 'That close to putting the Black Hole of Main Street out of business. And with your help . . .' He pinched his fingers together. 'Bang. *Sayonara. Hasta la vista* and *ciao*. Harold and Martha Peterson? You didn't reckon on the likes of Colin Ware, fresh from the land of 007, come to root out evil and corruption wherever he may find it.' Doug took a fresh complaint form from the folder. 'You dictate,' he said. 'I'll write it down and you sign it.' He picked up a pen from the side of the desk. 'Generations of artists yet unborn will sing praises to your name for what you're about to do here today, friend.' He placed the tip of the pen on the first line of the form and looked up to grin at Colin across the desk.

14

After his attempts to see her at Shining Shores, Colin was hesitant to call Mandy as he'd promised Joanie. Since her attitude toward him had obviously undergone a change – though only temporarily, he hoped – he didn't want to put her in the awkward position of having to manufacture an excuse to get off the phone, which would set things back farther than they already were. So rather than call, Colin decided to stop by her apartment, which she'd once pointed out when they were driving past it in her car.

He was able to find his way to her neighbourhood, and then it was only a matter of walking up and down two or three streets till he recognised her building, which he remembered was on a corner.

He walked up to its entrance, and looked down at the initials M M that were beside one of the doorbells. He glanced at his watch – he hadn't wanted to get there before she'd had at least an hour to relax after getting home from work – then pushed the button.

Mandy's apartment was on the first storey and when Colin reached the top of the stairs she was standing in her bathrobe just inside her doorway.

'Hello,' she said.

'Hi, Mandy.'

They looked at each other a few moments as Colin stood on the landing.

'Did you want to come in for a minute?'

'I hoped I could.'

She stepped back. 'I wasn't really expecting you,' she said, as Colin walked past her and into the room.

'I should have called.'

'That's what Joanie said you'd be doing.' She continued standing beside the open door.

'Joanie gave me Doug's name,' Colin said. 'Thank you.'

She shrugged. 'He was over at the Shores. I figured you might still be looking for people to draw.'

'I was.'

She nodded.

'That was very thoughtful.'

'Not really. He just happened to be out there.'

It was a small, single-room apartment and on all the walls and ceiling were stickers, and in a variety of colours, sizes and shapes, of butterflies. Colin looked at a few of them on one of the walls, then tipped his head back to see some of the ones above him.

'That's my symbol,' Mandy said.

'Butterflies?'

She nodded.

'They're nice.' He reached over to a particularly large black and yellow butterfly on the wall nearest him and picked slightly with his fingernail at the place where the edge of its wing was stuck to the wall. 'I guess when you leave they'll become your landlord's symbol.'

'Colin.'

'Mandy, could you close the door for one minute please. I'm not planning to stay.'

She closed it, but remained standing where she was, and again it was quiet.

'So how did it come out,' she said.

'What.'

'The drawing of Doug.'

'Oh. Very well. They seem to come out well when you choose the subjects for me.'

'I won't be choosing any more,' she said.

'You won't?'

'No.'

'Why is that.'

'Because I have to start getting on a new track,' she said.

He nodded.

'I have to start planning my future better. That's my biggest problem. I always just drift along from day to day. I'm not going to be that way any more.'

'No.'

'I'm going to be future-oriented.'

'Helping me find subjects won't fit into the new track.'

'It's nothing personal. I just won't have the time any more.'

'I can see that.'

Again, for a long time, it was quiet.

'Mandy, do you have to stand right next to the door?'

'It's my place, Colin.'

'I know that, but you're actually standing against the door.'

'Which I can do in my own place, Colin.'

He nodded again. 'True. In your own place you can stand against the door if you want.'

In the centre of the room was a low chair made of a red canvas fitted over curving iron rods. 'I take it that's a chair,' Colin said.

'A butterfly chair. Obviously.'

Again he nodded. 'I will say it's been good having Joanie around during this period.'

'What did Joanie do.'

'Nothing specific,' he said, 'I've just felt happy knowing she's there at the motel, even though I don't see her every day. You said her friendship meant a lot to you and I guess I can see how you feel about her.'

There was the sound of a car passing on the street. Mandy walked to the one window in the room and pulled down the blind, revealing another colourful large-winged insect pasted to the blind's inner side. 'Joanie said you've been going over to the library a lot.'

'Yes I have.'

'What have you been reading over there,' she said. 'Not that it's any of my business.'

'Magazines mostly.'

'Which ones. Not that it's my business.'

'Pretty much whatever's lying around on the table.'

Mandy was wearing a pair of fuzzy blue slippers. She walked in them across the room. 'Any particular ones you like?'

'Magazines?'

'I mean I'm really just trying to make small talk to be honest with you.'

'Well, that's better than no talk.' He looked down at the floor. 'Let's see. Earlier today I was reading a crime magazine.'

'Crime?' Mandy said, seating herself on the edge of her bed. 'I didn't realise you were into that.'

'I've always been very fond of crime.'

'So what kind of crimes were you reading about today.'

'Let me think.' He put his finger up to his chin. 'Oh yes. There was a case of a woman in Oklahoma who killed her husband, cut him up and fed him to his dog.'

'Whose dog.'

'The man's dog.'

'She fed him to his own dog?'

'Apparently. They had a picture of the dog.'

'How did he look.'

'I don't know,' Colin said. 'Sort of . . .' He shrugged. '. . . surprised.'

'I guess he would be.'

'Not the usual biscuit.'

Again it was quiet.

'So in other words, it sounds like you've been spending your time sitting around reading trash over at the library.' Mandy buttoned the large button on the bottom of her bathrobe.

'I couldn't have put it better myself.'

'For some reason I always thought you were a little more of a resourceful person than that.'

'I usually am.'

'I wonder why you're not these days.'

'I wonder too.'

Mandy's legs were crossed and one of her slippers was suspended on her foot above the floor. She began slowly turning it in a circle.

'When you're lonely,' Colin said, 'you sometimes tend to sort of drift along from day to day without being too resourceful.'

'I'm sure you're not lonely,' she said.

'I'm not?'

'How could you be. Like you said, Joanie's there. Vera's here now. You have your work to think about.'

They both watched her slipper turn slowly several times.

'What a whirlwind of fun for me,' Colin said.

'I'm not saying that. I'm just saying you have no reason to feel lonely. If you're telling yourself you're lonely because of something to do with me, I'm sure that's not the reason.'

'It's not.'

'No.'

'Well that's good to know,' he said, 'because that actually was one of the reasons I was giving myself.'

'It's not a true one.'

Colin stood looking down at the red chair a few moments. 'What if I sat on this,' he said.

'It seemed like you said you weren't staying.'

'I did say that,' he said, putting his hand on one of the curved fabric-covered supports, 'but I'm thinking of trying this out for a minute.'

'You've sat in those before, Colin.'

'I really haven't.' He stepped around to the front. 'You just basically lower yourself into it?'

'Stop acting like such an ass.'

He lowered himself into the chair, then settled down into the fabric pouch. 'I've done some pretty disreputable things in my life, Mandy, but lying about sitting in a butterfly chair is more contemptible than something even I would do.'

'I think you've tried it out now.'

'Very comfortable,' he said, leaning back in it. 'Kind of a sit-up hammock.'

'I think you get the idea now.'

'And I should be on my way.'

She nodded.

'And I will be,' he said, 'as soon as I make a little correction.'

'About what.'

'A remark of yours a couple of minutes ago.'

'Colin.'

He held up his hand. 'It'll only take a second.'

'Did you ever think I might not want to hear it?'

'You said my being lonely had nothing to do with you,' he said. 'It's just a tiny point, I'm sure we can clear it up in no time.'

Mandy looked back at her slipper. She stopped revolving it one way and began turning it the other.

'Then I'll be off.'

She nodded.

'So can we put that on the table?'

'Can we what?'

'Can we talk about that.'

'There's nothing to say about it, Colin. I can accept you might feel a little lonely about me. Because that's how I felt at first too.'

'You did.'

'It's perfectly normal at first.'

'Because before you said you were sure my loneliness had nothing to do with you.'

'And I could see why I said that,' she said, 'but I'll admit I might have been wrong.'

'You were.'

'The reason I said it was because since I'd gotten over what happened between us myself, I just thought you probably had too. But what I wasn't realising was it takes different people longer to get over those kind of things.'

'What kind of things.'

Her foot stopped again. 'You know,' she said, 'like when you have two people that think they like each other a lot.'

'Think they do.'

'Right. Then they might come to see it might have been just a physical thing or something and at first it's hard to move on with their lives. But they have to. So they do.'

'Just a physical thing.'

'I'm not saying that was true in our case,' she said. 'I was just using that as an example.'

'I see.'

It was quiet for a few moments, then Mandy got back farther on her bed so she could lean against the wall.

'I wonder how long it's going to take me,' Colin said.

'To what.'

'Stop missing you.'

'I couldn't tell you that.'

'As you say,' Colin said, 'it varies between people.'

'It does, yes.'

'Do you have any suggestions for me?'

'About not missing me?'

'Yes.'

'Just what I said before,' Mandy said. 'Start thinking of other things and start making future plans.' She turned her head to the side and reached up to separate some of her hair into a thick strand.

'That's good advice,' Colin said.

'It's all you can do, really,' she said, separating out a second wide strand of hair. She shook her head slightly to loosen her hair, then separated out a third strand.

'Can I give you an example,' Colin said, 'of a time that thoughts of the other person swept over me?'

'If you have to,' she said. 'I mean to be honest with you I'm not really that interested.' She began to braid the three long strands together.

'But it might give you an idea how to help me put the person out of my mind.'

'I said you could, Colin.'

'Yes. Well it happened this morning. I was at Doug's, at the Chamber of Commerce.'

She continued braiding her hair loosely together.

'And he wanted me to sign this complaint form,' Colin said. 'Do you know the little art shop on Main Street?'

'Petersons.'

'That's it.'

'That's where my butterfly stickers came from.'

'So you know who the Petersons are.'

'I knew their daughter when she ran it. She's the one who sold me the stickers.'

'Judy.'

'She went nuts last year.'

'Right,' Colin said, 'but Doug wanted me to sign a complaint form to help get them out of their shop. Apparently he considers them something of a blight on the community.'

Mandy moved the large braid up beside her face to try to see the part of it she had finished.

'But I didn't want to sign it. As important as I could see it was to him, I just didn't want to get involved in some political infighting here in New Cardiff. So I said I'd take a form along with me and think about it. But he was clearly annoyed with me. He'd been nice enough to sit for the portrait, and he was asking me sort of as a favour in return to help him out with his problem, and I felt very bad saying no, but on the other hand—'

'Colin.'

'Yes, Mandy.'

'Not to be rude, but in a way I don't see what this has to do with what we were talking about.'

'I'll tell you,' he said. 'The first thing – the very first thing – that happened as I came out of his office was I wished I could talk to the other person about what to do.'

She had braided the hair all the way down to the end. 'Can you toss me that rubber band?'

'Where.'

'There on the table.'

There was a table several feet in front of the chair. Colin leaned forward, reaching toward it.

'Don't worry about it.'

'I can get it.' The chair's legs scraped across the floor as he made several lurching motions in the direction of the table.

'I should have just got up and got it myself.'

'I have it.' He picked up the rubber band.

'Just toss it. You don't have to bring it.'

He threw it over to her, then pushed with his shoes against the floor till he'd moved the chair back to where it had been before.

'So in other words,' she said, 'you want to know what you should have done when you came out of Doug's office so you wouldn't have thought of me.'

He nodded. 'That's my question. What should I have done, there in the hallway of the Chamber of Commerce, so Mandy didn't flood into my mind for the hundredth time since I woke up this morning.'

'Hundredth time.'

'Ninety-ninth. Hundred-and-first. In that area.'

Mandy put the rubber band around her fingers, then transferred it to the end of the braid. 'I thought we were just going to talk about the one time.'

'That's true, I shouldn't have mentioned the others.'

241

'I'm not going to sit here and tell you a hundred different ways not to think of me.'

'I was getting greedy.'

'But actually the thing I'm going to tell you would work every time it floods in.' Mandy tipped her head back and looked at a butter-fly with green-and-blue wings directly above herself.

'I'm ready to hear it.'

'I know you're ready. I just in a way don't like to bring up personal things from your family life.'

'What family life.'

'You know.' She kept her eyes on the ceiling. 'Your parents and everything.'

'My parents.'

'Your father,' she said, 'to be specific.'

Colin looked up to see which butterfly she was studying, then back down at Mandy.

'He's the thing you should put your mind on instead of thinking of me all the time.'

'My father.'

She nodded.

'Whenever I find myself starting to think of Mandy, I should force myself to think of my dad instead.'

She lowered her gaze to Colin and nodded.

'That's an interesting technique. Is that what you did?'

'What.'

'When you were still thinking about me too much – you'd substitute your dad when I would come to mind?'

'I didn't do it. I'm saying you should.'

'But when we give advice,' Colin said, 'we usually base it on our own experience.'

'Right,' she said, 'but my dad's not having an operation.'

It was quiet a moment or two, then Mandy pointed at a clock on the same table where the rubber band had been. 'Could you just turn that to face me,' she said. 'I can't quite see what time it is.'

'I'll just tell you.' He looked at his watch. 'Ten to seven.'

'Thank you.'

'I'm glad to hear it,' Colin said.

'What.'

'That your dad's not having an operation.'

'Well I hope your dad's works out okay. I'm sure English doctors are just as good as American ones, so I don't think you should worry too much.'

Colin looked down at one of the struts of the chair coming up between his legs.

'And this is just my own opinion, but it really does seem like you should probably go back to England while he has it.'

For a long time he sat looking down at the top of the red canvas-covered support. 'Mandy?' he said finally.

'What.'

'I'm just trying to think back to when we had our discussion about my father's operation.'

'Well don't try too hard. We didn't have one.'

He nodded. 'That's probably why I'm having difficulty.' After another few moments he looked up at her again. 'So you didn't hear about it from me.'

'No.'

'Through the New Cardiff grapevine?'

'Colin, I think we both know who I heard it from.'

'All right. And did the source of your information also tell you what the operation is for?'

'No.'

'Well first let me ask you something else,' he said. 'Did this have anything to do with your leaving the motel?'

She shrugged.

'I'd like to know.'

'Yes,' she said.

'It did.'

'It sort of did.'

'And you have no idea what the operation's for.'

'Heart bypass or something?'

'Heart bypass you think.'

'Colin, I said I didn't know.'

'But since it's the entire reason you moved out – and you say "sort of", but it was obviously why you did – don't you at least think you should know what kind of operation it is?'

'Go ahead and tell me then.'

'I will.'

'It seems like you always have to beat around the bush about everything.'

Colin looked over at the small clock on the table for a moment, then back at Mandy. 'A year ago, my parents moved from one flat in London to another, to be a little closer to the store. And most of the furniture was moved professionally – sofa, beds and so forth – but some of the smaller stuff – an odd chair, pictures and such – they took to the new place themselves. And one item they took over was a wooden stool. And one afternoon my father was carrying the stool out of the lift in the new building. And accidentally he dropped it. And where did it land? On his foot. On his toe to be exact.'

Mandy reached up to pull the rubber band off the end of her braid.

'Well that toenail,' Colin said, 'of the toe he dropped the stool on, started kind of curling under, after that happened.'

She put her fingers into her hair to comb out the braid.

'My mum was after him for almost a year to see a doctor about it.

245

And finally, on her birthday, for her, he did. And what do you suppose he told him.'

'I wouldn't know.'

'Ingrown toenail.'

'Is that right.'

'And yes, they will have to operate. They'll have to remove the nail so the new one grows straight. Now as far as Dad's chances of recovery go . . .'

Mandy got up from the bed.

'. . . I would say they're fairly good.'

She went to the door.

'But whether the chances of recovery are as good for whoever's been supplying you with your information is something we'll just have to see.'

'We admitted two new residents today,' Mandy said, putting her hand on the doorknob, 'so I'm kind of tired, Colin.'

Colin placed his hand on the floor beside the chair, twisted around and put his other hand on one of the struts behind him as he tried without success to hoist himself up.

'That's why I don't sit in that too much.'

Finally he bent sideways, put both hands flat on the floor and crawled out of it, tipping it over.

'Could I ask you something?' she said.

'Of course, Mandy.'

'So she lied about the operation,' Mandy said. 'Well, not lied exactly, I guess.'

'I'm comfortable with lied.'

'But whatever you want to call it,' Mandy said, 'there was something else she told me too.'

'What was that.'

'About the way you met each other.'

Colin nodded.

'Your two mothers in the waiting room.'

'The Story.'

'That was true?'

'Unfortunately.'

'Not that it's important,' she said. 'You just like to know when someone's telling you the truth once in a while.'

'Vera's fond of telling people we met as foetuses.'

'Personally,' Mandy said, 'I wouldn't exactly call that two people meeting.'

'It's not a popular method.'

'But I guess she looks at it that way.'

'Social clubs where foetuses can get acquainted. Foetuses meeting through personal ads.' He shook his head. 'I agree with you. I don't see that catching on any time soon.'

Mandy opened the door, then it was quiet a few moments.

'Mandy.'

'I have to get ready for bed now. I know it seems early.'

'May I ask you something now.'

'What.'

'Do you have a passport,' he said.

'Passport.'

'A United States passport.'

'Colin,' she said, pulling the door open farther, 'I'm sorry to be rude, but I'm just really tired.'

'Do you have one?'

'No.'

'You don't think one might come in handy someday.'

'No.'

He looked through the door as a woman came out of the apartment across the landing and disappeared down the stairs.

'Because I went into City Hall. It's in the same building as Doug. I just went in to see how it's done here. It doesn't cost much. And they have a fast-track system so you can get one quickly.'

'Colin, I don't want one, okay?'

'But what harm would it do.'

'No harm. I just don't want one.'

'What would it take.'

'Take?'

'For you just to go over on your lunch break tomorrow and apply for one.'

'Colin, what part of "I don't want one" don't you understand.'

'But there must be something I can do so you'll get one.'

'There isn't.'

'Owning a passport doesn't commit you to anything, Mandy.'

'Colin, you need to get over me!'

'But I love you.'

She looked suddenly away.

'Forgive me for putting it in such a trite way,' he said, after a few moments had passed, 'but I love you with all my heart.'

She stood a long time with her hand on the doorknob looking out across the landing. Then nodded.

'What,' he said.

'There is one thing, Colin.'

'One thing what.'

'One thing you could do so I'll get a passport.'

'Tell me.'

'Just one.'

'What is it, Mandy.'

'If you will promise me,' she said, turning to look at him, 'that you will never come over here again. That you will never come out to Shining Shores. Never call me. Never try to see me again. Ever. In your whole life and in my whole life. Then I will go down tomorrow to the City Hall, since that seems to be so important to you, and send for a passport or whatever you have to do.'

'Yes, Mandy,' he said, nodding.

'Do you understand what I just said?'

'After I leave here now we're never going to see each other again.'

'Ever.'

'I understand the condition.'

'And you accept it.'

'Yes.'

'Because I don't think you really do.'

'I do, Mandy.'

'Our relationship is over,' she said.

'I accept that and I'll deal with it somehow.'

'Okay then.' She stepped aside. 'Goodbye, Colin.'

He walked past her and started down the stairs, but then stopped and looked back up just as she was closing the door. 'If I never see or talk to you again, how will I be sure you sent for the passport.'

'I'll figure out a way for you to know, Colin.'

He nodded, then started down the stairs again. 'Goodbye for ever.'

'And don't try to make a joke out of it, Colin.'

'No.'

'Because you might not think it's true, but you're going to find out it is.'

'Goodbye not for ever,' he said, continuing down. 'I mean goodbye for ever, but not saying for ever. Saying just plain goodbye, know-ing it's for ever, but not saying for ever because it sounds like a joke.' The door slammed behind him as he reached the bottom of the stairs.

15

CHAMBER OF COMMERCE –
VISITOR COMPLAINT FORM

Name: Colin Ware

Place of residence: London, England

Purpose of visit: Sketching New Cardiff inhabitants

Individual(s) whose behavior was displeasing (include
name of venue where incident occurred): Harold Peterson,
Petersons Art Supplies

Please use the rest of this page to go into as much detail as you can about the incident. Remember, as regrettable as your unfortunate experience was, you're giving us an invaluable tool to prevent it from happening to someone else in the future, and in doing that you're playing a vital role in the exciting story of an always-improving New Cardiff (your comments will be viewed only by authorised Chamber of Commerce personnel):

Because everyone here in New Cardiff has been hospitable to me in the extreme, going out of their way to accommodate me in every way possible, I'm highly reluctant to file this complaint against one of your residents. But if it will contribute toward New Cardiff becoming an even better place than it already is, I will state that Harold Peterson misrepresented a product to me.

The product was a pad of artists' drawing paper. The misrepresentation was that he told me the paper was acid-free (it's the acid content in paper that causes it to yellow over time, and this can be removed during the manufacturing process).

Since it is always designated on the paper whether it is acid-free or not, and since there was no drawing paper in Harold Peterson's shop with this designation, I asked if he had any, stressing its importance to me. I had to explain to him what it was, which seemed slightly odd to be doing to the owner of an art-supply store, and had I not been in a highly sleep-deprived condition at the time, I no doubt would have been more alert to this. In any case, though, he finally informed me all drawing paper now sold in the US is acid-free, and due to the well-known technological superiority of this country, I accepted this explanation as plausible and went ahead with the purchase.

About a week later, reviewing in my mind the circumstances of the sale, I began to feel nervous about the paper and I dialled the number of the company, which was listed on the front of the pad. I was greatly distressed to learn from the customer relations department that their company manufactures no acid-free paper.

As far as salvaging the situation involving my current drawings goes, I've heard of a product that can be sprayed on paper to reduce its acid content. So all may not be lost, and I will look into this when I've returned to England.

The second time Colin visited the Chamber of Commerce, Doug was in his office with a salesman, and motioned for Colin to enter when he saw him in the hallway. 'This is Colin Ware,' he said to the salesman as Colin came in, 'the renowned British artist.' He indicated for Colin to come closer. 'Show Colin.'

The man turned toward Colin. He was holding a necktie up so that it fell down across his chest, a depiction of the Battlefield Monument running the length of the tie.

'Don't say anything,' Doug said to the salesman. 'Let him form his own opinion.'

Colin looked at the man holding the top of the tie up against his neck.

'Tell us what you think,' Doug said.

Colin studied the picture on the tie, then nodded. 'It seems fine. It's a little lighter in colour than the real one.'

'That can be fixed,' the salesman said, turning back to Doug.

'Keep facing Colin.'

He turned to Colin again. The three men were quiet as Colin continued to look at the tie unfurled down the man's chest.

Finally Colin shrugged. 'I don't wear ties myself as a rule . . .'

'He's an English guy,' Doug said, stepping over to them. 'He's too polite to say it.' He took the tie from him. 'But he's thinking it.'

'Are you thinking it, sir?' the salesman said.

'Thinking what.'

Doug bent over slightly and held the top of the tie against Colin's belt buckle so that it hung down between his legs.

'You're wrong, Doug,' the salesman said.

'Just look at it.'

'Christ, Doug, no one wears their tie that way.'

'But if they did they'd be arrested for indecent exposure.'

'Mr Ware,' the salesman said, 'does the monument on that tie look to you like . . .' He frowned a moment, then looked down at Doug. 'What do they call them over there.'

'How do I know. Ask him.'

'You ask him.'

'Colin,' Doug said, looking up at him. 'Do they call them pricks over there?'

'That would translate.'

'Be honest, Mr Ware – is that what our monument looks like to you?'

Colin leaned forward slightly so he could see the design again on the tie hanging between his legs.

'Be honest, sir.'

'Actually it might have somewhat more of a flesh tone than the original.'

'Jury's spoken,' Doug said, straightening up.

'I'm telling you we can fix that.'

Doug handed him back the tie. 'You'll have people wearing these things out of their pants for a gag,' he said, guiding him through the door and out into the hall. 'Tell you what. Why don't you go back and have your people come up with one with a cannon on it.' He started back into the office, but then turned a final time to the salesman. 'But hold the cannon balls,' he called down the hallway after him. 'Those guys'll turn you grey if you let them,' he said, returning to the office. 'Take a chair, friend.'

Colin sat down, then reached into his pocket for a folded sheet of paper.

'What's this,' Doug said, taking it from him.

'The complaint.'

'You came through for me,' Doug said, seating himself at his desk.

'I did what I could.'

Doug unfolded the sheet of paper and sat quietly for a few moments reading it. He looked up at Colin when he was finished. 'So thanks to that bastard my picture's going to turn yellow.'

'Over time,' Colin said, pointing at the form, 'but as I mention in there, there may be a spray I can get.'

Doug swivelled in his chair slightly and tapped several keys on the keyboard of his computer. Colin glanced at the monitor on the desk as a list of telephone numbers appeared on the screen. Colin was about to say something but Doug raised his hand to silence him, then picked up the receiver of his telephone and pressed several numbers on the phone's keypad.

'What are you doing.'

'Sit tight, Colin, you're in good hands.'

Doug cleared his throat. 'Tom,' he said. 'Doug at the New Cardiff Chamber. Listen. I have another walking wounded down here from Petersons'. We're looking for a spray you put on drawing paper to get the acid out.' He listened a moment, then glanced at Colin and nodded. 'Overnight me a can of the stuff, Tom. Put it on our account. I owe you one.' He hung up the phone.

'Thank you, Doug, I appreciate that.'

'A classic work of art like the one you produced here the other day?' he said, leaning back in his chair and shaking his head. 'I'm sorry. Posterity and the progress of Western art aren't going to be

deprived of that experience by some retired heating-oil salesman with delusions of grandeur.'

'I'm happy you liked it.'

'Oh much more than liked it. Friend, you captured my very essence.' He looked out over Colin's head. 'Funny and serious all at once. Brash with just a hint of impishness. Pulsating with youthful energy while at the same time exuding a passionate sense of civic pride. God knows how, but you got it all in.'

'I may have to look at it again.'

'Now it's your turn to ask a favour,' he said, holding up Colin's completed complaint form. 'When I said you'd have the Key to the City in return for this, I meant nothing less.'

Colin nodded. 'Actually there is something.'

'Name it, Colin. A five-course dinner at the New Cardiff Grand?'

'No, there's just a question I had about the original Welsh settlers of New Cardiff.'

'That's all?'

'You were going to tell me about them last time, then we got side-tracked.'

'You're too easy.' Doug stood and walked across the room to a filing cabinet. 'Now this would be the original fourteen families we're talking about?'

'I learned a few things about them from Joanie at my motel.'

Doug pulled out a drawer of the cabinet. 'There's not that much to know,' he said, removing a folder. 'They came over and named the place. There wasn't any coal so they went down to Pennsylvania. I'm afraid that's as exciting as it gets.' He carried the folder back to the desk and sat down with it.

'There must be more known than that.'

'There's the journal,' he said, going through the papers in the folder. 'That's what I'm looking for. But that's about the best I can do for you.' He removed several pages stapled together.

'Journal?'

'The founder of the town kept it,' he said, handing it across the desk. 'The original's in the Statehouse up in Montpelier.'

Colin looked down at the top page of the photocopied document. It was written in small and careful printing, the lettering done in old-fashioned script with large curling Ss and Fs beginning many of the sentences.

'I had all the local merchants memorise a little spiel to rattle off when visitors show any interest,' Doug said, 'but I may put together a version of my own that has a little more sizzle than that one.' He sat a moment as Colin looked down at the journal. 'Wait a minute,' he said. He pulled his chair up closer to the desk. 'Colin. A brainstorm. Do something for me.'

'What's that.'

'Read a little of that out loud.'

Colin glanced up at him, then back down at the document.

'Would you?'

Colin shrugged. 'If you'd like.'

'Read it in an English accent.'

'I was planning to.'

'Go ahead. Take it from the top.'

Colin cleared his throat.

'Let me tell you what I have in mind first,' he said, raising his hand to stop him. 'We'll record the thing in your voice on cassette tapes and sell them in all the motels and gift shops around town.'

'Why would anyone buy that.'

'I'll tell you that part later,' Doug said. 'Just read it.' He leaned back, placed the ends of his fingers together again and turned his eyes up to the ceiling, but when Colin still didn't start reading he looked back down at him.

'I'd sort of like to know that part now.'

'I don't want it to affect the way you read it.'

'I'm sure it won't.'

'We'll say it's Winston Churchill.' He gestured at the document. 'Read.'

'Doug.'

'Bad idea,' Doug said.

'Very.'

Doug nodded. 'Scratch Winston then. But I do want to hear it in the accent.'

Colin looked back down at the journal and cleared his throat. '"On this day of Five September, Our Lord Seventeen Hundred and Forty-Seven, commenceth the Journal of Godwyn Edwards, Protector and Spiritual Leader of Sixty-Two Souls arrived on this Sacred Ground, named by our Elders New Cardiff".'

Doug was leaning back in the chair again, the tips of his fingers together as he listened.

Colin returned his eyes over the sentence he had just read. 'Edwards,' he said.

'Godwyn Edwards. He was Mr Big. A little later you'll be meeting Abigail, his wife. Don't get your hopes up, though, it doesn't get any steamier than it already is.'

'Edwards,' Colin said again, looking off at the wall.

For several seconds it was quiet.

Doug looked down at him.

'That's a very common Welsh name,' Colin said.

'I wouldn't know.'

After a few more moments Colin handed the document across the desk to him.

'That's it? That's all I get to hear?'

'I'd like to talk about the Key to the City.'

'It's yours, friend.'

'Anything I want.'

Doug returned the journal to the folder. 'Well. Within bounds.'

263

'What bounds.'

He closed the folder and looked back at Colin.

'What bounds,' Colin said again.

Doug set the folder down on the desk, then placed his hands on top of it. 'Shrewd judge of human nature that I am,' he said, 'I sense we're about to have revealed here the dark side of Colin Ware.'

Colin nodded. 'We are,' he said. 'I'm just hoping the Key to the City has a dark side as well.'

16

It was just before eight o'clock when a knock came on the door of number twelve and Colin opened it to find Joanie outside. 'Were you going to bed?' she said.

'Watching *The Godfather*.'

'We're watching the special on killer bees.'

'It was a hard choice.'

'They've migrated up to Maryland already,' she said, 'and they're expected here next summer. But you'll be gone by then.' She rested her hand on Colin's wrist. 'Mandy just called.'

'Mandy?'

'I memorised her message,' Joanie said, frowning down at the walkway at her feet. 'Let's see, "Everything's been sent off. It will be back in seven business days".' She looked up at him again.

'"Everything's been sent off. It will be back in seven business days",' Colin repeated.

'That's word-for-word.'

Colin felt his shoulders sag slightly as they relaxed. 'Thank you, Joanie. Thank you very, very much.'

'And Colin,' she said, 'this is none of my business, I'm not trying to butt in – I didn't say anything to Mandy about this – but I was quite surprised at someone as up-to-date as she is about these things going about it in this way.'

'Going about what.'

'Maybe back when I was a teenager we did it like this, Colin. But now you just go down to the drugstore, bring something home to dip into your pee, it turns this or that colour and you know in five minutes.'

'If you have a passport?'

'What?'

'Oh, oh, if you're pregnant.'

'I mean I don't know about England,' Joanie said, 'but Mandy of all people is someone I would expect to be aware of the latest methods. Anyway, Fisher was trying to figure out how many days you've been here.' She removed her hand from his wrist so she could count on her fingers. 'I don't think you've been here long enough for her to start worrying just yet, Colin.'

'No.'

'Although I don't know if having a little Colin or Mandy running around the place would be all that bad either.' Joanie opened her arms. 'Let me give you a great big New Cardiff hug.' Colin stepped out the door and she put her arms around him. 'Oh we're so happy to have you here,' she said, rocking back and forth slightly as she embraced him. 'I can't tell you how delighted we all are to have you here.'

'No more than I am, Joanie, to be here.'

'You're such a nice person.' She held him a few moments longer, then stepped away. 'Is this the original *Godfather* you're watching?'

'I didn't come in at the beginning.'

"See you tomorrow, Colin.' She turned around and hurried back toward the sliding door leading into their living quarters. Colin stepped into his room again, closed his door and returned to the bed. He fluffed the pillows that were piled against the headboard, rearranging them more comfortably, then got on the bed and settled back and read the final credits of *The Godfather*.

Colin had just washed out the one pair of socks he'd brought to America and was draping them over the shade of a bedside lamp to dry more quickly when the phone rang. It was Vera. 'I have to see you,' she said, 'but I don't want to come to your room this time.'

'How about the Deep Cup,' Colin said.

'What's that.'

'It's across the street.'

Colin was already seated in a booth when Vera arrived at the diner ten minutes later. 'No socks either?' she said, looking at his bare ankles as she approached the table.

'What's on your mind, Vera.'

She slid in on to the seat across from his. 'Colin, you are not going to believe what happened this afternoon.' She looked over at the waitress behind the counter. 'Miss?' She raised her hand. 'A tea please?' She turned back to Colin.

'I've ordered.'

'Colin, you are not going to believe what I'm about to tell you.' She opened her bag and removed an envelope. 'I don't even know how to start. Let me start with Doug.'

'Doug.'

'You did his picture.'

'Oh that Doug.'

'Reed?' she said, opening the envelope. 'Something like that. Anyway, he called me up this afternoon and asked me to come over to the Chamber of Commerce.'

'I think I mentioned you in passing.'

'Well it was more than in passing, Colin. He seemed to know quite a bit about me. That I'm half Welsh, among other things.'

The waitress came to the table and set down a cup of water and a tea bag in front of Vera, and a piece of pie at Colin's place.

'This is what you've got to see.' Vera removed a sheet of paper from the envelope as the waitress walked away. 'This is what you won't believe.' She set it on the table between them. 'My family tree.'

'Really.'

'Going back three hundred years. Doug went to the website of that place in Salt Lake City that has everybody's genealogy in the world.' She moved his plate slightly so she could put the piece of paper directly in front of him. 'You can just type in a credit card number and get your family tree. So he got mine.'

'Amazing,' Colin said, looking down at it.

'And I know I keep saying you won't believe this, but I guarantee you it's the most incredible thing that's ever happened.'

He picked up her tea bag and dropped it in her water. 'Vera, I'm already getting tired of this subject and I don't even know what it is yet.'

She put her finger on the bottom of the page. 'Okay. Here I am. You see my name.'

'Vera Edwards.'

She moved her finger over slightly. 'And here's Alicia.'

He nodded.

'Here's Dad,' she said, pointing to her father's name, 'and the person he married.'

'Your mother.'

269

'Right.'

'I knew who he married.'

'It's set up with these lines linking up all the marriages and children. It's a little confusing.'

'I still knew who he married.'

She moved her finger up a little higher on the page. 'And here's Grandma Edwards. This is her maiden name in brackets. Which is spelled wrong.'

'That's not how you spell it?' Colin said, turning his head so he could read it.

'It's Kendal,' she said, 'with just one "l". Then you go up here.' Vera moved her hand over the names in the middle of the page. 'I've never heard of most of these people. Just various ancestors. But you wind up here.' Her finger had come to rest on one of the names at the top of the page.

Colin looked at the name. 'Godwyn,' he said.

'Godwyn Edwards.'

'Don't know that many Godwyns.'

'This is the part you won't believe.' She moved her finger to the name next to Godwyn's. 'And this is Abigail, his wife. Try to guess who these two people are.'

'I can't.'

'Try.'

He shook his head.

'Try, Colin.'

'Adam and Eve? I give up.'

Her finger remained between the two names at the top of the page. 'Godwyn and Abigail Edwards are the people who founded New Cardiff.'

Colin sat quietly looking down at her family tree.

'Don't you get it?'

'I guess I don't.'

'Colin, the people who founded this town are my ancestors.'

Colin looked at her a few moments without speaking. 'Come on,' he said finally.

'I swear to God.'

'No.'

'I know. I can't believe it either.'

He looked down at the names, then at her again.

'It's true, Colin.'

'You're related to the people who started this place?'

'There's even a journal written by this person Godwyn,' she said, picking up the sheet of paper. 'I have a copy of it back at the motel. It's a good thing I don't believe in fate or I'd think the whole reason everything has worked out the way it has was just so I'd come over here and find this out.' She put the paper down on the table again. 'But that's just the beginning.'

'No more revelations, Vera, I couldn't handle them.'

'Doug wants me to promote the town.'

'New Cardiff?'

'Yes.'

'How would you do that.'

'He has a whole strategy worked out for me, Colin. And get ready for this promotional gimmick. He wants me to be queen.'

'Queen?'

'Of New Cardiff.'

Colin sat silently a few moments looking across the table at her. 'Queen of here.'

She nodded.

'Queen Vera of here.'

'You should have heard him go on about it. "You're a living legacy. You're the human embodiment of the hopes and dreams of all New Cardiffians, past, present and future." Well I don't have to tell you how he talks.'

'It's known as jabbering.'

She lifted her tea bag out of the cup by its string and set it down on her saucer. 'But I mean really – this is too absurd. Even for me.' She took a sip of the tea. 'This is lukewarm.'

'Even for you,' he said.

'I do tend toward bizarre behaviour, as you know,' she said, 'but this is over the top. I mean don't you think?' She set her teacup back down.

'Queen Vera,' Colin said, looking at his pie.

'I could never do this.'

'What would your duties be. You'd have a crown?'

She shrugged. 'I'm sure he'd come up with some sort of queen outfit. There's an annual Fall Festival next month. I'd preside over that. The local merchants would be photographed with me for ads. He says the motel owners would all be falling over themselves to give me a free room. But really, Colin, this isn't something you think I should seriously consider, do you.'

'It could take over your life.'

'They'd actually hire me for this. The town would actually pay me. Oh, and I'd promote their water, that's another thing he wants me to do.'

'I drank some of that.' Colin pulled a napkin out of an aluminium holder at the side of the table.

'He wants to build an ad campaign around me when they start marketing it. TV spots and personal appearances around Vermont.'

'You'll definitely need a crown for that.' He set the napkin in his lap.

'God, you should have heard him on this subject. Walking around his office, waving his arms in the air.'

'Doug gets excited.'

'He wants to put my picture on the label. At one point he even said he thought it should be called Queen Vera's Water.'

'He might want to rethink that touch.'

'I should hope so,' she said. 'But Colin. Seriously. I really don't know how to turn him down without hurting his feelings. Because he is kind of nice. So I can either tell him I'm flattered, but I don't have the time, or I can be honest with him and say it's just too ridiculous.'

'Nice,' Colin said.

'What?'

'You think he's nice.'

'For a crazy person, I would say he is.'

Colin picked up his fork.

'But Colin, please tell me whether or not to do this.' She reached into her bag for a pack of cigarettes, then glanced at the waitress and dropped them back in again.

'You seem highly agitated.'

'I am, Colin. Help me.'

Colin took a bite of his pie. 'What about Vera's Treasures.'

'Then there's that.'

'Would you keep it?'

'I don't know. Gemma's been trying to buy me out for the last two years. In one way I'd be well rid of it.'

'Gemma.'

'You know, she has the little framing stall next to me.'

'So they'd become Gemma's Treasures.'

'Colin,' she said, placing both of her open hands on the table in front of her, 'I know we have major differences right now. And I don't know how to resolve them yet. You don't either. But I have absolutely no one else to turn to for advice, so won't you please put our problems aside for now and just be totally honest and help me make this decision.' She sat looking across the table at him. 'I'm so torn about this. I don't even know why.'

Holding his fork a few inches above the plate, Colin looked down at his pie, but instead of cutting himself a piece he just sat staring at it as Vera watched him.

'Colin?'

He remained motionless, not looking away from his plate.

Finally she reached over and ran one of her hands back and forth in front of his eyes. 'Earth to Colin,' she said. 'Come in if you're receiving.'

Colin lowered his fork to the table. 'I can't do this.' Again it was quiet for a few moments. 'I can't go on with it.'

She was frowning at him.

'I'm not this kind of person,' he said. 'I'm not a hidden agenda kind of person.'

'You're not what?'

'It's a hoax,' he said.

275

'What is.'

He picked up her family tree from the table. 'This. It's all a fake.'

Vera glanced down at her tea, then back across the table at Colin. 'You're making no sense.'

'You've been duped.'

'Duped.'

'The Queen of New Cardiff,' he said. 'My idea. I thought of it.'

'Doug thought of it.'

Colin pointed at himself. 'I came up with the queen part. Doug thought up the family tree angle.'

She looked at him a moment longer, then held up her hand to the waitress. 'My water wasn't hot. Can you bring another cup?'

'It's all a fraud, Vera.'

'Colin, I don't understand why you're saying this.'

'Because I was very pissed off at you. For one thing I found out what you told Mandy. About my father's operation, as you called it.'

She nodded. 'I mentioned that to her.'

'That he's preparing for a life-threatening operation.'

'Not in those words.'

'You implied it to her, Vera. Come on. The man's having an ingrown toenail removed.'

'There could be complications.'

The waitress appeared beside their table with a cup of hot water. 'Is this what you wanted?'

'Please.' She pushed her other cup out of the way.

'Did you want another tea bag?'

'Just the water.'

The waitress set the cup down and walked away.

Colin watched Vera put the old tea bag in the new cup of water.

'I saw a way to revenge myself on you. For tricking Mandy into moving out of the motel. For the Roger Pelham bullshit you put everybody through.'

'Revenge.'

'But I'm not a vengeful person,' he said. 'I wish I was. I must have a character flaw.'

'Colin,' she said, taking the family tree back from him, 'why are you telling me you had anything to do with this.'

'What?'

'It's very distressing what you're saying.'

He nodded. 'I know it's distressing.'

'So why are you saying it.'

'Guilt,' he said.

'But why are you telling me the queen idea was yours.'

'I just told you. Guilt. I couldn't keep up the pretence.'

'Colin,' she said, 'I'm totally baffled.'

He watched her dip the bag up and down in her cup.

'Why do you want me to believe this wasn't Doug's idea?'

'Because it wasn't.'

'Colin.'

'Vera, you're saying you don't believe I made this up?'

She took a sip. 'Of course I don't.' She returned the cup to its saucer. 'Because you didn't.'

'Vera.'

'Why are you doing this.'

He looked back at her, but without speaking.

'Your attitude is very odd, Colin,' she said, 'to say the least.'

'You really don't believe I'm behind this.'

'You've always been a very bad liar.'

He picked up the sheet of paper again. 'Kendal,' he said, finding her grandmother's name. 'With one "l". That's why it's misspelled. I thought it had two. I wrote down as many of your family's names for Doug as I could think of and I spelled that one wrong.'

'Colin, why are you trying so desperately to take credit for his ideas.'

'Credit?'

She removed the sheet of paper from his hand, folded it and

returned it to its envelope. 'This is incredible,' she said, putting it back in her purse. 'I've never seen this side of you before.'

'Vera, the whole thing is a fake. Listen to me.'

'I suppose Doug didn't go on the Salt Lake City website.'

'He didn't.'

'And I suppose I wasn't standing behind him looking at his monitor the whole time he was doing the search.'

'You may have been standing behind him,' Colin said, 'but he loaded all that into it in advance.'

'The whole Salt Lake City database of everyone's genealogy in the world.'

'He got their home page up, copied it, then put it in there somehow along with the stuff I told him about your family.'

'Really.'

'I watched him do it.'

She kept looking across the table at him a few more moments, then began to nod. 'I've finally got it.'

'Got what.'

She continued to nod. 'It just registered.'

'What did.'

'I've been sitting here, racking my brains, trying to work out why you're doing this. And it's so obvious. You're jealous.'

'Jealous.'

'You don't even know it.'

'Of what?'

'That this is happening to me,' she said. 'You wish it was you.'

'Vera, if I had wanted to be the Queen of New Cardiff I would have thought it up for myself.'

'You're pathetic.'

He shook his head. 'Vera, please try to focus on this.'

'You wish all this was happening to you.'

'Vera.'

'Be honest.'

Colin looked up at the ceiling. 'I don't know how to get it over to you.'

'Colin, you could never have thought up something like this.'

'Why not,' he said, looking back down at her.

'You just couldn't have.'

'I did.'

'You couldn't have.'

'I did.'

'You were talking before about Doug jabbering,' she said. 'Now who's jabbering.'

'I'm confessing.'

'Just please stop this.'

'Vera.'

'I mean it, Colin,' she said, holding up her hand. 'It's making me feel kind of sick.'

It was quiet as they looked across the table at each other.

'Will you?' she said finally.

'Of course, Vera.'

'Thank you.' She removed the tea bag from the water, quickly squeezed it over her cup and set it on the saucer. 'Because I want to tell you the rest of what Doug said.'

Colin cut a small piece of his pie. 'I'll stop jabbering. Tell me the rest.'

'If I do decide to go through with this,' she said, 'I'll tell you the main reason that I will.'

He raised the bite to his mouth. 'Alicia,' he said.

'What?'

'I didn't say anything.'

'Right. Well if I turn down his queen offer, Doug says he'll fly Alicia over to do it instead. As he pointed out, as far as ancestry goes she's as qualified as I am.'

'"If all else fails, Doug,"' Colin said quietly, '"say you'll call her sister. You'll have her. I'll guarantee it."'

'What?'

'Nothing.'

'What did you say.'

'Nothing. I coughed.'

'I heard you say something.'

'I coughed and burped at the same time.'

She looked at her cup. 'Where was I.'

'Alicia.'

'Right,' she said. 'God. Talk about my worst nightmare. Can you imagine little Miss Conceited, prancing around for the rest of her life, rubbing everybody's nose in the fact that she was once Queen of New Cardiff, Vermont?'

'Annoying.'

'Not annoying.'

'Insufferable.'

'There isn't a word, Colin, so don't try to find one.'

He took another bite of the apple pie. 'So now it sounds like you may not be abdicating.'

'If it means Alicia will be ascending, I just may not be.'

They sat quietly, Vera taking several more sips of her tea as Colin finished his pie. Then Colin coughed.

'You might be coming down with something,' Vera said.

'I might.'

'Maybe you should get back.'

'Probably.'

Vera looked over at the waitress. 'I think we're finished,' she said.

Colin nodded. 'I think we are.'

A final visitor came to see him before Colin was able to go to sleep. He had just turned off the light and was settling down under the covers when he heard several loud knocks. At first he thought it might be on the door of the adjoining room, so he waited without saying anything, till after a few seconds it came again. 'Who is it.'

'Colin? Open up.'

He waited another moment, then got out of bed and pulled on his trousers. 'Doug?' he said, putting on his shirt and buttoning it as he went to the door. He opened it to see Doug standing in front of him.

'Two words,' Doug said. He held up two fingers on one of his hands.

They stood a few seconds looking at each other.

'Two words,' he said again.

'What two words.'

'Class act,' he said, lowering his hand.

'What about it.'

'Hardly the Brit bimbo I was led to expect, friend. Hardly. And let me tell you this – you're a very fortunate fellow to have diplomatic immunity. If you were one of our folks, a fist would be saying hello to a nose at this point in time.'

Colin stepped out through the door, closing it partially behind him. 'Doug.'

'Are you following me?' Doug said.

'Not that well.'

'Let me bring it down to one word for you then.'

'One.'

'And that word is Vera.'

Colin nodded.

'Are you with me yet?'

'You're saying I gave you the wrong idea of her.'

'Big time.'

'That I called her a Brit bimbo? No, Doug.'

He patted the side of Colin's arm. 'You might as well have, friend. but let me set you straight on something else while we're at it.' He raised his hand again, this time to point at Colin's face. 'When she walked through my door this afternoon, and I saw the quality human being I was dealing with, there is no way in hell I would have gone through with your tacky little scam if I didn't consider my word to you – as I consider it to all my fellow-creatures – my sacred bond.'

Suddenly the window of the room beside them was pushed open

and a man with rumpled hair scowled up. 'Could you conduct this brilliant conversation elsewhere?'

'Our error,' Doug said. 'Forgive our thoughtlessness.' He walked between two parked cars and across the car park to the fence surrounding the pool, then waited as Colin followed him gingerly in his bare feet. 'Sixty grand a year they pay me to get these people here,' he said, as Colin joined him, 'and you've got me dragging them out from between the sheets in the middle of the night.'

Colin leaned against the fence, lifting his leg to brush something off the sole of his foot.

'Oh, and while we're at it,' Doug said, putting his fingers up against his lips and making a sucking sound, 'what's this all about.'

'What.'

'This.' He made the sucking sound against his fingers again.

'You'll have to be more specific.'

'They used to call me Old Yellowfinger,' Doug said, 'so don't tell me I haven't been there. But when I saw that shimmering vision of grace and elegance reach into her purse for a pack of those, I scratched my head.'

'We're talking about Vera's smoking now,' Colin said.

'I'm still scratching it.'

'If that is what we're talking about, she is trying to give it up. As usual.'

'And that's good enough for you, isn't it.'

'That she's trying to give it up?'

'For God's sake, friend, help the woman.'

'I do,' Colin said. 'I discourage it.'

'Discourage it.'

'Doug, people do make their own decisions about things.'

Doug held his hand out in the direction of the motel office. 'This paragon of beauty and intelligence is killing herself before his very eyes, and what does he say? "I discourage it." God in heaven, tell me I didn't hear that correctly.'

In the wall of the pool, underneath the surface, a large light turned the water blue. Colin held his wrist at an angle so he could read his watch from it. 'I have to go in now,' he said, 'but there's been a development.'

'What development.'

'I blew the whistle on us.'

'You what?'

'I told her the whole thing was a fake.'

'She knows?'

'Not exactly. After I came clean, she still believed it.'

'She did?'

'She thought I was lying about making it up.'

'I was that good?'

'You must have been.'

'But that doesn't please me,' Doug said, looking down at the ground. 'To have deceived a virtuous and trusting woman makes me feel like that gum wrapper there at your feet.'

'I'm going in, Doug.'

'Don't leave me out here.'

'I have to,' he said, turning around.

'One last thing.' Doug put his hand on Colin's arm to stop him. 'I didn't tell you what she said as she was leaving.'

Colin turned back toward him. 'Doug, I need sleep.'

'We were standing out in the hallway. I'd just made some pleasantry about hoping she was enjoying America. And then she said it.'

Colin waited several seconds for him to continue. 'Said what, Doug. Hurry.'

'She kind of looked off down the hallway,' Doug said. 'And in that incredibly musical voice of hers, she said, "I wish Americans wouldn't smile so much."'

Again it was quiet. 'Americans wouldn't smile so much,' Colin said.

'Yes.'

'May I go in now?'

'Let me tell you the rest of it. She said, "I wish Americans wouldn't smile so much. It makes them look so sad."'

Colin glanced down at Doug's hand on his sleeve for a few moments, then removed it.

'God, what a perceptive woman.'

'Goodnight, Doug.'

'I may have conned her on one level,' Doug whispered loudly after him, as Colin picked his way slowly back across the car park in his bare feet, 'but on a deeper one she saw through me like a plate of brand new glass.'

Colin stepped into his room, then looked back at Doug, still beside the pool where he had left him. 'She wants to do it,' Colin said. 'She wants to be Queen of New Cardiff.'

Doug held his arms out beside himself and looked up at the sky. 'Oh, Colin,' he said, 'that terrible yet wondrous thing the poets have sung about down through the ages has finally found its way into the lonely heart of Douglas Elmore Reed.'

Colin looked at him a few moments longer. Then he closed the door and slipped the security chain into place.

17

Dear Mandy,

Due to our agreement we won't be seeing each other
again, and though I wish I hadn't made that promise, I
know you wouldn't respect me if I went back on it.

So let me say it's been a great pleasure to know you, and
you've made my stay here in New Cardiff a memorable
one. I'll always look back fondly on the times we had
together, and hope you'll give my best to your brother
Rob.

Your friend,
Colin

PS Coincidentally, I've just heard from a cousin of mine who's touring the States at this time. Cheswick's more or less the black sheep of the family, which is why I didn't mention him before.

But he's visiting Washington DC now, and plans to come up to New England after that. Unfortunately, I'll be gone by the time he gets here and won't be able to show him around.

Any chance you could spend a little time with him? I told him to be at the library Saturday morning in case you had a minute or two to stop by and try and pick up his spirits.

I don't know exactly how to describe Cheswick. I've been told we look alike but I shudder to think it's true.

Being a Saturday, the New Cardiff Public Library was crowded, with a group of children sitting on the carpet in one corner as a woman read to them, several high school students studying, some older New Cardiff residents looking at newspapers and various patrons coming in and out to return the books they'd finished reading or to check out new ones.

After coming through the entrance, Mandy stopped beside the front desk and stood a few moments looking at Colin, on the other side of the room. Then she walked over to the table where he was sitting. She stood across from him till he looked up. It was quiet a moment, then Colin closed his magazine and set it on the table. 'Are you Mandy?'

'I guess you're Cheswick.'

'Yes,' Colin said, holding out his hand.

She shook it. 'You do look a little like your cousin.'

'Sad to say.' He continued to hold her hand as they looked at each other.

'You've been in DC then.'

'I have.'

'Sightseeing?'

'This and that.' He kept her hand in his.

'Colin wrote me that you were down there.'

'An odd chap, that cousin of mine, didn't you find?'

'Colin's a little odd.'

'Very peculiar.'

'I don't know if I'd go that far.'

They looked at each other a few more moments, then glanced at a woman seating herself at the end of the table.

Colin indicated the chair across from his. 'Don't you want to sit down?'

'Maybe for a minute.' Mandy pulled the chair out and sat.

The woman at the end reached into her purse for a pair of glasses.

'So let's see,' Colin said, 'I'm trying to think what Colin said you were doing these days. Didn't he say you were waiting for a passport to come through?'

'He might have. He said I should probably have one when he was over at my place a week ago.'

'I wondered if it came through.'

'It did,' she said. 'Did you want to see it?'

'Yes, I enjoy looking at people's passports.'

Mandy reached into the back pocket of her Levi's and removed her passport. 'The picture came out pretty well,' she said, handing it to him.

He opened it and looked inside. 'Very well.'

'My driver's licence picture always comes out well too.'

'Really,' Colin said, giving it back to her. 'Most people's don't.'

'I'm just the opposite.' She returned it to her pocket. 'It's all the other ones that never turn out.'

The woman at the end of the table opened a book, touched the end of her finger to her tongue and began going through its pages.

'Let's see,' Colin said. 'I'm trying to think what Colin said you were doing these days.'

'You might have already said that.'

'Oh yes, so I did.' It was quiet a few moments. 'Oh I know what I was going to ask you, that's right. Didn't Colin say something about how you were thinking of going back to England with him at one point?'

'At one point,' she said.

'Is that plan still on?'

'Not if he went back without me.'

Colin nodded. 'Unpredictability,' he said, 'that's always been Colin's biggest problem. But what surprises me is that last time we talked he mentioned some business opportunity he'd heard about over there.'

'In England?'

'Right.'

'Well that's probably why he went back. So he could do that.'

'Not for him,' Colin said. 'For you.'

'For me?'

'A business opportunity over there for you.'

She frowned. 'I'm sure he didn't say that.'

'No, he did.' Colin smoothed the cover of the magazine on the table in front of him. 'He definitely did. Apparently he wanted to be certain when you got there you'd have enough to do. So he got his friend to help him find you a job.'

'A friend over there?'

'One here,' Colin said. 'Didn't you introduce him to some fellow at the Chamber of Commerce?'

'Oh, Doug.'

'That's who it was. He and Doug went on the Internet and turned up a job opening at some seaside town.'

'But for me?' she said, pointing to herself.

'You are Mandy.'

'Yes.'

'That's who it was for.'

'Well what could it be?'

'At some home over there, I think it was.'

'Home?'

'A retirement home.'

'What?'

'I know what it was.' Colin held up his hand. 'Now I remember. A home for retired bus conductors.'

She looked at him a few moments, then shook her head.

'Bus conductors,' he said again.

'What are they.'

'They sell you your ticket on the bus. But I don't think they have them as much as they used to.'

Mandy looked down at the picture of a man behind bars on the cover of the magazine in front of Colin.

'Anyway, he and Doug were searching websites for job opportunities over there, and they ran across an employment notice for someone to take over this place because the last managers had been mistreating the residents.'

'Mistreating them.'

'Right.'

'The retired bus conductors?'

'Apparently.'

'How could you do that.'

'Mistreat them? Same way you'd mistreat retired schoolteachers or retired firemen, I suppose.'

Mandy watched him smooth the magazine cover again. 'Look, Colin. Could we not do this Cheswick stuff any more?'

'Cheswick stuff.'

'I mean it was amusing at first,' she said. 'But I think it's getting a little old.'

'Could we do it just a little longer?'

'But I'm trying to find out what you're talking about.'

'And you will,' he said, 'but could we do the Cheswick stuff one more minute.'

'I guess if you insist.'

'Thank you.' He reached into the pocket of his shirt. 'Now. Did Colin tell you anything about my hobby?'

'No, Cheswick.'

'He didn't.'

'No, Cheswick. What's your hobby.'

'Jewellery collecting,' Colin said, bringing out a small white envelope. 'He didn't tell you that?'

'No, Cheswick.'

'I guess it slipped his mind,' Colin said, removing a small ring

295

from the envelope, 'but that is sort of my passion. Here's something I ran across in a jewellery shop down in DC the other day.'

'What's that.'

'Just a little ring.'

She waited a moment, then leaned across the table to look at it.

'Just a little gold ring,' he said, 'with a little butterfly on it. Nothing much. But I saw it and I just went ahead and bought it on the spot. I couldn't help myself.' He held it for a few moments as Mandy studied it. 'That's how I am when I see a piece of jewellery I like. Impulsive.'

The woman at the end of the table glanced down at them, then back at her book.

'You can hold it,' Colin said.

'I don't have to.'

'Go ahead.' He gave it to her.

'There it was,' Colin said, 'sitting in the glass case. I took one look at it and . . .'

'It's not real gold though.'

'Excuse me?'

'It's not made out of real gold.'

'It's not?'

'I mean I'm asking.'

'I won't go near costume jewellery.'

She inspected it more closely. 'And what are those.'

He pulled his chair up to the table so he could lean across to look more closely at it himself.

'In its wings,' she said, pointing to it.

'It has a little ruby in each wing,' he said.

'Those are rubies?'

'The little red stones.'

'But they're not real.'

'They'd better be.'

'Those are actual rubies?'

'Actual.' He nodded.

Mandy held it closer to her face. 'And you just saw it in a case?'

'There it was, mixed in with a couple of dozen other rings and watches and bracelets, and I just saw it and I said, "I'll take it." Just like that.'

'So what kind is it,' she said.

'Kind?'

'Like a friendship ring or something?'

'Oh, what kind. Well I did ask the jeweller that. And he said it was an engagement ring.'

'Engagement.'

'Which surprised me,' Colin said. 'I said, "I didn't think engagement rings looked like this. I thought they were sort of silver,
maybe with a diamond or something in them."'

'That's what I thought,' Mandy said, looking up at him.

Colin shook his head. 'No. He said they can be any way people
want them to be.'

'I guess that's the latest thing,' she said, looking back at it.

'Those were his very words. "It's the latest thing now," he said, "for
people to just have them be any old way they want."' Colin sat
quietly a moment as she continued to examine the ring. 'Of course
there was one very disappointing thing about it.'

'What was that.'

'It's used.'

'It is?'

'Second-hand. I was leaving DC and I took it out to look at it and
I noticed it was used.'

'It has a scratch on it or something?'

'I almost went back and returned it,' he said, 'but the train was
leaving the station and I figured . . .'

'But I mean how could you tell it was used.'

'Because it has the last people's names in it.'

'It has what?'

'If you look inside,' he said, 'two names are engraved in it, who
must have been the last people who owned it.'

298

'Where.'

'Hold it up and look on the other side of the butterfly. They're very small, but you can make them out. They're in a little heart.'

Mandy turned it at an angle, to get more light on it, then squinted as she looked inside.

'See the names? I forget what they are.'

For a long time she held it perfectly still next to her eyes, then suddenly she sucked in her breath, let it out and drew in another deep breath.

'Mandy?'

She pushed the ring on to one of her fingers, then again sucked in a deep breath.

The woman at the end of the table looked up over her book.

'Mandy,' Colin said.

Mandy put her hand on her chest, just below her neck, and took several short breaths.

'Let's remove this,' Colin said, taking her hand with the ring on it.

She shook her head, pulling her hand away before he could remove it, and sucked in more air.

'What's wrong with her,' the woman said.

'Mandy.'

'She's hyperventilating,' the woman said.

Colin took one of her hands in both of his. 'Mandy.'

Her chest rose up and down as she continued gulping air.

Taking off her glasses, the woman at the end of the table stood up. 'Could we have some help here! We have an emergency!'

'Mandy,' Colin said, rubbing her hand between his.

'I'll be okay,' she said between breaths.

'We need help here!' the woman yelled.

Colin glanced over toward the corner. The children had stood up and turned around. The woman who had been reading to them hurried in front of them and motioned for them to sit back down.

'Mandy?'

Her eyes were closed. 'Just give me a minute.'

'Here come the librarians,' the woman said.

Colin looked up to see a man and a woman hurrying toward the table. 'What's happening.'

'She just started hyperventilating,' the woman said.

The man stepped over to Mandy. 'Can you hear me?' he said.

'Yes,' she said.

'Are you going to lose consciousness?'

'I don't know.'

'I don't think she is,' Colin said.

'Who are you.'

'Her fiancé.'

Several other patrons had begun to move toward the table.

'Margaret,' the man said, 'get them back.'

'Go about your reading,' she said, motioning them away. 'She needs air.'

Suddenly the man began sweeping books and magazines off the table and on to the floor with his arm.

'What are you doing,' Colin said.

'Get her on her back on the table,' he said. 'Margaret, call a doctor.'

'No doctor,' Mandy said, waving her arm through the air, her eyes still shut.

'Lay her on her back,' the man said to Colin. 'I'll take her legs, you take her shoulders.' He bent down and grasped Mandy by the ankles. 'Hurry up, man.'

Colin put his arms around Mandy's shoulders.

'Have you got her?'

'Yes.'

The man kicked the chair away, then hooked his arm around Mandy's legs and hoisted her up. 'A doctor,' he said to the other librarian.

'She doesn't want one.'

'Call one, Margaret.'

'What if she's Christian Science,' Margaret said. 'Liability.'

'Are you?' the man said, putting Mandy's legs down on the table.

'What.'

'A Christian Scientist.'

'I don't know.'

'She is,' Colin said. 'Don't call a doctor.' He rested her back and shoulders carefully down on to the table.

'You,' the man said, pointing to the woman at the end of the table. 'A book to put under her head.'

The woman bent over and began going through the books he'd pushed off the table.

'Has this happened before?' the man said to Colin.

'Not that I know of.'

The patrons had not obeyed Margaret's request to return to their seats, and in fact several more had come to look curiously at Mandy lying on her back on the table.

'You,' the man said, pointing at a white-haired patron holding a newspaper at his side several yards away. 'Go to the medical section and find me *Layman's Guide to Health Emergencies*. I believe it's by Morrison, Albert.'

'I really wouldn't do that,' Margaret said.

The woman at the end of the table was holding a book out to him that she'd picked up from the floor.

'What's her name,' the man said to Colin, as he took it.

'Mandy, but I think—'

'Mandy,' the man said, 'we're going to use this book as your pillow.' He held it up in front of her closed eyes. 'You're going to be all right.'

Still sucking in her breath, Mandy let her arms fall beside her on to the table.

'Where's the medical section,' the man with the newspaper said.

'Margaret, show him.'

She shook her head. 'I won't, Victor, I'm sorry. It's for your good too.'

'Well do something!'

Margaret turned and started away.

'Now where are you going.'

'I'll get *The Life of Mary Baker Eddy*.'

'I might take her out of here,' Colin said.

'Oh no. Don't move her.'

'Yes, take me out.' Mandy raised her arms again.

'You don't want to be moved, Mandy.'

Mandy put her arm around Colin's neck. Colin reached under her shoulders and put his other arm under her legs and lifted her up from the table.

'Sir,' the man said, 'this is the very worst thing you could be doing for her.'

'I want him to,' Mandy said.

'I'm chancing it.' Colin hoisted her up slightly higher and started toward the door.

'Here,' Margaret said, coming up to Colin with a large book.

'I don't have a card.'

A small boy separated himself from the other children and came toward them. 'Is she dead?'

'Not yet.'

Another patron held open the front door as he carried her out of the building and down toward the street. 'How do you feel.'

'I just started gasping,' she said.

'But is it better.'

'I think so.'

'Can you open your eyes yet.'

She opened them.

'Good,' he said. 'Are you in the library car park?'

'Rob has my car.'

'You don't have your car?'

'His is in the shop. He borrowed mine.'

Colin stopped when they reached the sidewalk, turning to look one way then the other. 'Which is closer,' he said, 'your apartment or my motel?'

'You can put me down now, Colin.'

'I want to carry you.'

'But I'm better.'

He started down the sidewalk with her. 'I'm experiencing an atavistic urge to carry you.'

'Not all the way to the motel.'

'My manhood's crying out to meet its supreme challenge. I'm sorry if it seems primitive.'

She was quiet as he carried her down the sidewalk and past a bank.

'Really, Colin.'

'I can't help it.'

Ahead of them Harold Peterson had stepped out of his art supply store and stood on the sidewalk, watching them approach.

'I drew him two days ago.'

'Mr Peterson?'

'I felt so guilty about filing the complaint against him I came over and drew him from across the street. I was going to show him the drawing to try and make things up, but I don't think it would have.'

'Hello,' Mandy said as they reached him.

He continued staring at them but without speaking.

'Say hi to Judy when you see her,' Mandy said, looking at him around Colin's arm as they continued on.

'He glowered,' Colin said. 'He knows what I did.'

'That's how he always looks.'

Colin carried her to the corner, stopped to wait for the light to change, then stepped into the street and started across.

'Well Colin?'

'Yes.'

'When you were Cheswick, you were talking about the retired bus conductors. Was that true?'

'There are six of them in the home.'

'Well how did the people who ran the place mistreat them.'

'Didn't feed them,' Colin said. 'Generally neglected them.'

'That was on the Internet?'

'A social services number was on the website,' he said, stepping up on to the opposite kerb. 'Somebody there told me a couple named Croft was supposedly taking care of them, only they used their food allowance to have drug parties with their friends while the residents were sitting hungry in their rooms. I guess it was a big scandal in the town when it came out.'

'What town was it,' she said.

'Brighton.'

She shook her head.

'You haven't heard of it.'

'What's it like.'

'Beautiful. I've always wished I could live there myself.'

They walked quietly for a few moments.

'Aren't I getting heavy?'

'We're building a memory.'

They went past a drug store.

'Well who's running the place now.'

'They have a temporary person in there for the moment,' he said, 'but if they don't find someone permanent, they'll have to close it down.'

'I'm sure they won't just put them out on the street.'

'They'll find new places for them,' Colin said. 'But that's their home. They've all lived there together for years.'

Mandy looked down at the sidewalk in front of them. 'But what would I do there. Just basically the same things I do at Shining Shores?'

'You'd run it.'

'I'd what?'

'Run it.'

She looked at him without speaking as they passed a beauty parlour.

'Manage it,' he said.

'I couldn't do that.'

'You couldn't manage it?'

'Be in charge of this place?'

'That's the whole point,' Colin said.

'How could I do that.'

'You'll have staff to help you. I'll help.'

'Staff.'

'Employees.'

'How could I have staff,' she said.

'How?'

'Under me?'

'I guess you could put it that way.'

'But how will they know what to do.'

'Obviously you'll tell them,' he said, 'unless you want them wandering aimlessly about.'

A man and woman stepped off the sidewalk for a moment so he could carry her past.

'Will the staff be English people?'

'More than likely.'

'Colin, I couldn't order English people around.'

'What difference does that make.'

She shrugged. 'I just couldn't.'

'Practise on me.'

Mandy kept her eyes on the sidewalk in front of them as they walked. 'What if I tell them something to do and they don't do it. What happens then.'

'You fire them.'

She looked up at him. 'Colin, I could never fire someone.'

'I suppose you'd give them a payrise.'

'Really,' she said. 'How could I ever do that.'

'You'd start by calling them into your office.'

'My office?'

He carried her through another intersection. 'Reach down to my pocket, my side pocket, for a letter.'

Mandy put her hand into his pocket and pulled out a folded piece of paper. 'This?'

'Open it.'

'What is it,' she said, shaking it to try to open it.

'A fax,' he said. 'It came to the motel. I gave them that fax number.'

She reached around his neck to open it all the way with her other hand.

'It's to you,' Colin said.

'Me?'

'Read it out loud.'

She held the letter in front of her face as he carried her. 'It's in handwriting.'

'It's what?'

'I thought faxes were in typing.'

'Mandy, just read it.'

'Can't you tell me who it's from?'

'One of the residents.'

She waited a moment, then cleared her throat. '"Dear Miss Martin."' She looked away from the page. 'Miss Martin.'

'That's your name.'

'Are they going to call me Miss Martin when I get over there?'

'It's your name. Why shouldn't they.'

She shrugged and looked back at the letter. '"Dear Miss Martin, Mr Alford at social services has informed us of the interest you've expressed in our plight."' Again she paused, looking at the sentence she had just read.

'Mandy, just read it through without stopping.'

'I didn't express interest in their plight.'

'We can discuss that afterwards.'

She nodded. '"Just when all seemed lost",' she read, '"to hear that our desperate situation had come to your attention has brought

311

renewed hope to us here, and it is not an exaggeration to say that our senior member, Mary McMullen, has begun eating properly again after all of us feared her despondency would surely overwhelm her.'" Mandy turned her head to say something to him.

'Just finish it, Mandy.'

She looked at the letter again. '"The acts of generosity and kindness that have marked your distinguished career in America . . ."' She frowned.

'Go on.'

'Who wrote this letter anyway,' she said, looking at the bottom. 'Hugh Church.'

'Distinguished career,' Colin said. 'Go on.'

'What is that.'

'Your distinguished career?'

'Yes.'

Colin shrugged.

'Did you tell them something like that?'

'Mandy, just get to the end. You're heavier when you're not reading.'

She looked back at the letter. '"Mr Penrose-Smith recalls reading about one of your charitable crusades through Texas last year, but unfortunately didn't save the newspaper." Colin, did you tell them I did charitable work in Texas?'

312

'That was in the newspaper, Mandy. You're not even listening to yourself.'

'But how could it be in the newspaper if I didn't do it.'

'It must have been a misprint.'

'"In fact",' Mandy read, '"when Mrs McMullen got better, she said she thought you must be an American angel, flying over here on golden wings to rescue us."' Mandy began shaking her head. 'Oh no.'

'Oh no what.'

'This is terrible.'

'Why.'

'Because they have completely the wrong impression of me.'

'Mandy, thanks to you the woman started eating again.'

'But their hopes are getting up too high. What if I get over there and she stops.'

'She won't.'

'They think I'm some kind of great person.'

'The Crofts locked them in their rooms and wouldn't turn on the heat in winter. How hard an act is that to follow.'

They were walking past a car dealership, with many small, coloured flags strung across the used cars parked on the lot in front of the showroom.

'Colin, do you really think I could do something like this?'

'They're all waiting for you over there, Mandy. Waiting and watching the skies.'

Joanie was in the office looking over the guest register when she happened to glance up and see Colin carrying Mandy along the other side of the highway. She watched them a moment, then picked up the receiver of the phone, quickly pushing a button on the keypad. 'Fisher?'

By the time she'd hung up Fisher was in the doorway that led from their apartment. He turned his head in the direction his wife was looking, then stood watching Colin carry Mandy past the car park of the Deep Cup Diner. 'What in hell's that about.'

'Go help, Fisher. He's struggling.'

Fisher hurried out the door of the office, waving his arms over his head to them as he approached the highway. Several cars and a large truck passed, and he walked quickly across to Colin and Mandy.

Joanie watched as he spoke to them. At one point he held out his arms to take Mandy, but Colin turned and kept hold of her. Fisher said a few more words to them, then stepped forward into the highway, holding up his hand to stop a car so Colin could carry her across. Fisher walked beside them through the motel car park, reaching into Colin's pocket as they approached room number twelve to take out the key card and open the door for them. Mandy took the card back from him as Colin carried her inside, then the door was closed and Fisher came back to the office.

'Well?' Joanie said, as he came in.

'They're engaged.'

She looked over at Colin's room, then back at Fisher. 'Are you serious?'

'They just did it,' he said, walking past her.

'Well why was he carrying her down the highway.'

'It's a custom where Colin comes from.'

'To carry her along the side of a highway?'

'Roadway. Highway. Whatever.'

She looked back at him without responding.

'It's from an ancient Druid ritual, Joanie. Apparently they carried their intended down a long path as a symbolic way of embarking on the path of life ahead of them.'

'Where'd you get this.'

'Colin.'

'He told you that?'

Fisher straightened some brochures in the display case. 'He explained it as we were walking along.'

'He was putting you on.'

'No he wasn't.'

'A Druid ritual? Fisher, give me a break.'

'That's why he didn't want any help. If he successfully carries her all the way to their destination, without setting her down, it means they'll have a long and happy future together.'

'And you bought all this of course.'

'Nothing to buy, Joanie.'

She walked back around the counter. 'You're hopeless.'

Fisher watched her turn to a new page of the register. 'You know something, Joanie.'

'Totally hopeless.'

'No,' he said, 'but I am deeply saddened that your cynicism prevents you from appreciating and sharing in the joy of a colourful custom from a foreign land.' He walked to the door of their apartment, but then stopped, resting his hand on the knob and looking down at the floor.

'Are you stuck?' she said finally.

'What?'

'Are you stuck or something?'

'I'm sad, Joanie. I told you that.'

'That I'm so cynical.'

'Yes.'

'Well I just remembered another old Druid custom,' she said.

'What's that.'

'What they used to do to the people in their group who weren't particularly bright.'

They stood quietly looking at each other.

'And it wasn't pretty, Fisher.'

After a few moments he reached up to adjust a plaque on the wall slightly, then went back into their apartment.

Next time Joanie glanced up, Mandy was at the window of room twelve. When she saw Joanie looking at her she smiled and held up her hand, pointing at the new ring on her finger. Joanie silently formed three words with her lips. They laughed, then Mandy reached over to pull the curtain across the window as Joanie's attention returned to the guest register.

Part III

18

Mary McMullen loved the video from America, and had watched it at least once a day since it had come. Even on Excursion Day, after lunch, when everyone else was getting ready for the trip to Brighton Pier, she slipped into the lounge to see it again.

Sitting in the worn green armchair, her hand resting on the remote control in her lap, she read the words VT PROMO – QUEEN V. on the television screen, then watched as the familiar image of Queen Vera appeared, seated beside a table, wearing her short-sleeved, abbreviated red-and-white robe, the small gold crown resting on her head. Mary studied Vera as the camera moved slowly in closer to the familiar image, then as Vera turned and

321

said, 'Hello. I'm Queen Vera, and I reign in the beautiful little village of New Cardiff, Vermont, a place where everyone feels welcome, a magical place where yesterday and tomorrow meet.'

Mary glanced quickly at the doorway of the lounge.

'But I'm not here to tell you about the many wonderful things you'll see when you visit me in New Cardiff,' Queen Vera said, as Mary looked back at the television, 'which I hope will be very soon. No, today I want to tell you about something you won't see when you come here. Something way deep down in the ground underneath my peaceful village.'

'A spring,' Mary said.

'A spring,' Queen Vera said, as the camera pulled back from her. 'But not just any spring. A very special spring. One that nobody even knew was down there till just last year.'

'Mrs McMullen.'

Mary turned to see Mandy in the doorway of the lounge.

'The others are waiting out in the van.'

'It's almost over.'

Mandy looked over at the television as Queen Vera raised a glass of water to her lips and drank. A contented smile spread across her face. 'The first time I tasted this delicious spring water I wasn't sure it was water at all. I thought it must be some delicious elixir from a mystical kingdom far beneath the surface of the earth.'

'Mrs McMullen,' Mandy said.

'It's almost over, Mrs Ware.'

'Now I'm not going make any irresponsible claims for this amazing water,' Queen Vera said, 'and I'm not promising anything like this will happen to you, but after a very good friend of mine had been drinking two or three glasses of it a day for a month – oh, and I should mention that she was a life-long smoker – she woke up one morning and all her nicotine cravings were gone. And guess what – she hasn't had the desire for a single cigarette since then.'

'I think I might know who her good friend is,' Mandy said, walking across the room.

'Oh please, Mrs Ware.'

'In a minute I'm going to ask my geologist to come out and explain the scientific reasons for the sparkling and health-giving qualities of this unique beverage.'

Mandy reached toward the television.

'Oh Mrs Ware.'

'It's not almost over, Mrs McMullen, she hasn't even sung the water song yet.'

'But first I want to show you one of the life-size Queen Vera cut-outs to be looking for in your supermarket next week.'

Mandy clicked it off. 'You can watch the rest when we get back.' She went over to Mary, set the remote control on the table, and took her hands.

'Mrs Ware?' she said, as Mandy helped her up from the chair. 'Is Queen Vera coming to see us next month?'

They walked slowly across the room together. 'She and her friend Doug will be here on the fifteenth, and everybody can talk to her and get acquainted.'

'When I meet her I'm going to tell her what lovely eyes she has.'

Mandy stepped aside so she could go first.

'Do you know Queen Vera?' Mary said, as she went through the doorway and into the hall.

'I met her once.' Mandy pointed toward the front. 'Mr Ware has the van out this way.'

'And didn't you tell me she lives in a big hotel? I'm trying to remember the name of that.'

'The New Cardiff Grand.'

'That's right. And is it very beautiful?'

'It's very nice.'

'And does she go down into the village sometimes and talk with the people?'

They continued down the hallway. 'Do you need to go to the bathroom before we leave?'

She shook her head.

'Are you sure?'

They went slowly past the living room. 'Just one more question.'

'I'm happy to answer your questions, Mrs McMullen, but we shouldn't make the others wait.'

'I think you told me Queen Vera's coming over here to visit Wales.'

'She's going to the Cardiff in Wales to try and get tourists to travel back and forth between the two places,' Mandy said, walking ahead to open the front door for her, 'that's right.'

'And will she bring me some water?'

'Mr Ware called her specially to be sure she brings you a bottle.'

In the van, parked just by the door, Colin was sitting behind the steering wheel, with the other residents on the seats behind him. 'We're itching to go,' he said, watching as the two of them came out, then as Mandy tested the front door of the house to be sure it was locked and walked with Mary across the driveway and helped her up on to the seat next to Colin.

'We're itching.'

'I heard you, Colin. She was watching the Vera tape again.' She carefully shut Mary's door, then opened the one behind it. 'Can someone scoot over for me?

'Where are Jennifer and Frank,' Mrs Wynter said, moving over.

'They're having their day off,' Mandy said, getting in beside her. 'They'll be back by dinner. Seat belts everyone?' As the others pulled theirs on, she reached to the front to help Mary McMullen with hers.

Colin started the engine and backed out of the drive and into the street.

'Oh, Colin,' Mandy said, 'I hope you aren't going that shortcut way again.'

'I was.'

'Because everyone had a stiff neck when we got there last time.'

As Colin started forward, Mandy turned so she could see the others in the van. 'I want to quickly go over what we're going to do when we get to the pier,' she said. 'Mrs Campbell?'

'I'm listening.'

'Mr Ware will drop us off in front, then he'll go find a place to park, and I thought we could all have a doughnut while we were waiting for him.' She raised her hand. 'Could everyone raise their hand who wants a doughnut?' She looked around at the others as they lifted up their hands. 'So everyone wants one?'

'Mr Ghandi doesn't,' Mrs Campbell said.

'Mr Ghandi?' Mandy said. 'You don't want one?'

He shook his head.

'Why don't you,' Mrs Campbell said.

'None of your business.'

'When we get out of the van,' Mandy said, lowering her arm, 'we all need to stay close together while Mr Ware parks.'

Mrs Campbell turned in her seat to look behind her at Mr Ghandi. 'Can't you answer a friendly question today?'

Mr Ghandi gestured for her to turn back around.

'Here's something we never did before,' Colin said, bringing the van to a stop at a crossing.

'One second, Colin. Now the only other announcement I have is that there are always lots of teenagers on the pier. They run around and half the time they don't look where they're going. Last time Mr Church was almost knocked down. Do you remember that, Mr Church?'

'Yes, and I also remember waiting for an apology that never came.'

'Right. So always try to be aware of unpredictable teenagers, Now are there any other questions before we get there?'

'I don't like the ingredients,' Mr Ghandi said.

'You what?' Mandy said.

'Don't like the ingredients.'

'Okay, well that's not really a question.'

Colin drove through the junction.

'Mrs Campbell asked me why I don't want a doughnut.'

'It has nothing to do with the ingredients,' Mrs Campbell said. 'He just likes to be different.'

'Go to hell,' Mr Ghandi said.

Colin glanced into the rear-view mirror. 'Mandy.'

'One more second, Colin. Mr Ghandi, we don't talk to women that way.'

'She is no woman.' He looked out his window.

'I'm sorry, Colin,' Mandy said, looking toward the front again, 'what were you saying?'

'Actually it was a bad idea.'

'Well what was it.'

'I thought we could all sing.'

'Sing?'

He veered sharply to avoid a car double parked at the side of the street.

'Careful, Colin.'

'I don't know what I was thinking.'

'I'm not against it. But I mean what would we sing.'

'That's it.'

'What songs would we all know.'

'There's probably not a bus conductors' anthem.'

The street running past the entrance to the pier widened so that taxis and other vehicles would be out of the way of passing traffic when they were discharging passengers. Colin pulled over and stopped by the kerb and Mandy got out and went around to open the doors of the van for the others. 'Colin?' she said, as they were getting out. 'Do you want me to take your things for you while you park? So you don't have to lug them back?'

He looked out at her from the driver's seat.

'Your sketch pad and everything.'

'I don't have them.'

'I thought you were bringing them.'

'You suggested it. But I didn't.'

The man in the car behind Colin beeped.

Mandy helped Mary McMullen the rest of the way down on to the kerb. 'We'll be over by the archway.' She closed the door and Colin drove away.

By the time he'd parked the van and walked back, the doughnuts had all been finished and the residents were standing at the side of the pier, looking down at the people on the pebble-covered beach below.

'Colin?' Mandy said, going up to him as he approached.

'I finally had to park underground.'

'Could I just say one thing?' she said.

'Say many things.'

'Just one,' she said, taking his hand, 'because I was kind of nagging you before about not bringing your art things. And I know ever since Jeremy came to dinner I've been sort of pestering you about your drawing. And I shouldn't.'

'You're concerned,' he said, 'that's not pestering.' He glanced over at the others. Mr Church was calling down to someone on the beach below.

'But it's sort of not my business, is it.'

'Mandy, everything's your business.'

'It's just that Jeremy made such a big point of wanting extra drawings in the back to show people during your exhibit.'

Mr Church put his hands on the railing and leaned forward. 'Are you man enough to come up here and say that?'

'He'd like more. But it's not essential.'

'But wouldn't you like to have some more?'

A stone came up over the railing and fell onto the pier at Mr Church's feet.

'Not necessarily.'

'And Colin?'

'Mandy, I don't like to see you worrying about this.'

'But the last drawing you did was the one of me a few months ago,' she said. 'And I keep thinking it's my fault you can't do more.'

Mr Church bent over, picked up the stone and threw it back down at someone on the beach.

'A supervisory vacuum's developing,' Colin said.

'You know that news-stand where we were last week and I said you should try to draw the man there? And it didn't come out because you said there wasn't enough light?'

'Not that there wasn't enough,' Colin said. 'The light quality was wrong.'

'Because I was in there again yesterday,' she said, 'and the light seemed fine.'

Colin pointed at Mr Church, who was crumpling up an empty paper cup, preparing to hurl it at someone below. 'Escalation in progress,' he said.

Mandy let go of his hand and turned around. 'Mr Ware's back,' she said. 'Let's all come over here now. Mr Church?' She shook her head.

'It's distressing how the quality of visitor to the beach has deteriorated since I first began coming here,' Mr Church said, dropping the cup in a bin.

The residents walked across the boards of the pier to join them, except for Mr Penrose-Smith, who remained beside the railing. He lifted up his foot.

'Is that gum?' Mandy called.

'Bubble gum.'

'How does he know that,' Colin said.

'We'll take it off later,' she said, 'but right now we have to move along.'

In a group, they started toward the arcade, Mrs Campbell glancing up at a loudspeaker as they passed it. 'Why must they play that wretched music so loudly.'

Mandy and Colin fell several yards behind. 'So it's not a problem that you're not drawing then,' Mandy said.

Colin shook his head. 'I could turn out a drawing a day and Jeremy wouldn't be satisfied.'

Ahead of them, Mr Penrose-Smith picked his shoe up several feet off the pier every time he took a step.

'Struggle to the arcade as best you can,' Colin said. 'I'll scrape it off there.'

'And I shouldn't feel guilty that you're not.'

He took her hand and raised it up to his lips. 'Mandy, you should never feel guilty about anything.'

Mr Penrose-Smith went over to a brightly flashing horse-racing game just inside the entrance of the arcade, steadied himself against it and held out his foot to Colin as he came in. 'You'll need something stiff,' he said. 'Perhaps a credit card would work.'

Colin removed his wallet, going through several of the cards before selecting his Visa.

On their last visit to the pier, Mrs Wynter had become highly agitated playing one of the games, but as soon as she entered the arcade this time she went right back to the same game and started playing it again. It was a glass-windowed booth with shelves inside where prizes were displayed between mounds of coins, and as more coins were dropped into a slot at the top the prizes were slowly nudged forward so they would fall into an opening below.

Mandy stood watching as Mrs Wynter fitted several coins into the slot, looking in at the prizes as each coin fell, then quickly inserting the next. When they were gone she removed a five-pound note from her purse, fed it into a change machine beside her, scooped up the new coins and started pushing them into the slot.

Mandy walked slowly over beside her.

'The watch,' Mrs Wynter said, pointing through the glass to a silver watch at the edge of one of the shelves. 'It's almost ready to fall.'

'This happened last time, Mrs Wynter.'

She dropped in another coin.

'I told you before – they just make it look like it's going to fall so you keep putting in more.' Mandy opened her own purse and removed an envelope. 'Look. I brought this to put your money in today. Then I'll give it back to you later.'

Mrs Wynter made a fist as she looked in at the watch. 'Almost.'

'Don't put any more in,' Mandy said, holding the envelope in front of her. 'Here.'

She dropped another coin.

'Mrs Wynter.'

'Please don't stop me.'

'But last time you almost had a nervous breakdown.'

Mrs Wynter shook her head and put in another coin, then another, but as she dropped the next one in the coins on the shelf moved forward slightly, pushing something off the edge.

She kept looking through the glass for a moment, then turned to Mandy. 'I won.'

'Well see what it is.'

She reached down into the opening to bring up a small doll and hold it between them.

'Homer,' Mandy said.

'What?'

'It's a Homer doll.'

'Homer?'

'Simpson.'

'Oh.' Mrs Wynter stood quietly for several seconds studying it.

'So you don't have to do it any more,' Mandy said. 'You don't have to put any more money in.'

'No.'

'Are you sure?'

'Yes.'

'Positive?'

Mrs Wynter nodded, continuing to look down at the prize in her hand. 'Thank you, Mrs Ware,' she said finally. 'I'll be all right now.'

Colin was still standing by the horse-racing game, breathing on his credit card, as Mandy walked up to him. He rubbed it.

Mandy watched him breathe on it again. 'What are you doing.'

'These can lose their magnetic charge if you abuse them.' He frowned at the brown strip on the back. 'It might be gum damaged.'

'Colin?' she said. 'Remember what we were talking about before?'

He held up the card to examine it in more light.

'That you've stopped drawing? Because sometimes I think it's because you got married.'

He shook his head.

'It isn't?'

'Some artists go for years without doing any work,' he said. 'I really wish you wouldn't keep worrying about this.'

'Years?'

'It's common with all creative people. I read about a poet who wrote one poem in his whole life.'

'Really?'

'He was quite happy to have written the one.'

'I wonder what it was about.'

'His mother as I recall. And I think it was even a haiku.' Colin looked across the room, then at his credit card again. 'I'm going to make sure this still works. I'll be right back.'

'Well, Colin?' she said, as he started away. 'I mean you're not saying that could happen to you.'

'What.'

'Not draw any more.'

'Oh no.'

'I hope not.'

He looked at her a moment longer, then walked off between the games and toward a snack bar.

While they were talking, Mandy had noticed Mr Ghandi, who was in a booth in the centre of the room, and after Colin left she walked over to the booth and looked in at him, seated in front of a large screen on which animated monsters were rushing back and forth. She put her head into the booth. 'Mr Ghandi?'

He looked up at her.

'Did you want some help?'

'Why would I want help, Mrs Ware.'

'Because you're just sitting there. I don't think you know how to play the game.'

They looked back at the screen. One of the monsters was racing forward and hurling boulders at them. 'Here.' She put Mr Ghandi's hand on a plastic handle in front of him. 'Shoot him.'

'Why.'

'What?'

'I have no desire to shoot him.'

'That's the whole point, Mr Ghandi. Otherwise they kill you.'

'Of what importance is that.'

A scaly green monster was lurching toward them, beams of fire shooting out of its eyes. Mandy took the stick from him, aimed the gun and pulled the trigger. The monster screamed and blew up. 'Did you see how I did that?'

He didn't respond.

'Mr Ghandi?'

She looked at him a moment longer, his hands folded in his lap as a two-headed snake hissed, uncoiled and leapt at him. Then she shrugged and backed out of the booth, making her way to the exit of the arcade where everyone was to congregate after half an hour and continue down toward the end of the pier to the rides and other outdoor attractions.

When Mandy reached the doors the only other member of the group who was there was Colin, holding a small paper plate with a pastry on it.

'What's that,' she said, going up to him.

'A scone.'

'A what?'

'They make them so people can find out if their credit cards are working.'

She picked it up and took a small bite. 'Stale,' she said.

He nodded. 'A stale scone.'

She removed the plate from his hand, carried it over to a bin against the wall and dropped it, along with the rest of the scone, inside. 'Do you feel better now?'

'I didn't know I felt badly.'

'I was just hoping you were feeling better,' she said, coming back to him, 'since we started talking about your art. But, Colin? Can I say just one final last thing about it?'

'Mandy, how many ways are there to bring up that I'm not drawing.'

She shook her head. 'It's not about that. I mean, it's partly about Jeremy, but not about not drawing.'

Colin shrugged. 'Whatever helps.'

'It's about after Jeremy left that night he came to dinner.'

Colin nodded.

'Do you remember that?'

'After he left,' Colin said. 'Not too well.'

'I'm sure you wouldn't,' she said. 'I mean, I even had to put you to bed.'

Several feet away was a large window that looked out to sea. Colin stepped over to it and leaned back against the ledge at the bottom.

'Do you remember anything about that night?'

Colin looked down at the floor. 'Waiting for Jeremy to come, I remember that. The bell ringing.' He nodded. 'Going to the front door. Jeremy telling me there was a case of wine in his boot that was a gift from an artist who owns a vineyard in Provence.' He looked up at Mandy. 'Then I remember the next day.'

'So basically you don't remember anything you said in bed that night,' she said, coming over to sit against the window ledge beside him.

'Not basically.'

'Not at all.'

He shook his head.

'Because you said some things I've been thinking about ever since.' She rested her hand on his knee. 'And I've been kind of afraid to bring them up again.'

'I can see why you would be.'

'Why.'

'Because I'm sure they were gibberish.'

'Can I tell you?'

'You can,' he said, 'but I already know they weren't comments we'll want to carve in stone.'

'You kept saying I didn't need you any more.'

He nodded. 'We won't need the chisel for that one.'

'You said I'd found my family now, with the others, and if you disappeared it would probably take me a week to notice you were gone.'

'Look, Mandy.'

'You did say that.'

'I'm not disputing I said it. But I'm wondering why the words of someone who couldn't even get up a flight of stairs unaided would stick in your mind as a memorable quotation.'

They sat quietly for a few moments, looking down at her hand on his knee, till finally he rested his hand on top of hers.

'That all my love was going to Mrs McMullen and Mr Ghandi and the others now and you could feel that there wasn't any left over for you.'

'A new conversational rule,' Colin said. 'When we're discussing the comments of someone who was unable to find their way to bed, those comments will not be given the same weight as the speech of persons who can find their way to bed.'

'If you didn't mean any of that, Colin, why were you crying when you said it.'

He removed his hand from the top of hers. 'I was pissed out of my mind that night, Mandy. When people get pissed they blubber and spout rubbish.'

'They say the truth.'

'They say the opposite.'

'Then what about that day at the Battlefield Monument,' she said. 'Just after we met. Why was getting drunk the only way I could say to you how I felt then.'

He shook his head. 'Altogether different.'

'It wasn't, Colin.'

Mrs Wynter and Mr Penrose-Smith had come to wait by the exit door, standing several feet from each other, facing in opposite directions.

'It was the only way I could express my true feelings,' Mandy said, 'so don't say people don't tell the truth when they're drunk – or pissed, if you want to call it that – because that's exactly what they do.'

Colin glanced over at Mrs Wynter. 'They're gathering.'

Mandy turned to see Mrs Campbell walk past the other two and toward the door. 'We're going to wait inside till everyone's here,' she said, getting to her feet.

Mrs Campbell went back to stand with the others. 'I hope you haven't forgotten your promise last time about the photograph, Mrs Ware.'

'We'll do it on our way back.'

'It's to be an Easter gift for my twin grandsons in Glasgow.'

'I'm aware of that, Mrs Campbell.'

A long stretch led from the arcade to the end of the pier where the rides and other attractions were, and it was as they were walking along that section that Mr Church began comparing Mandy and Colin unfavourably with the former managers. 'The Crofts may have had their faults,' he said, staying behind with the two of them as the others went ahead, 'but they never objected to my going on the Turbo when we came to the pier.'

'From what I've heard about them,' Mandy said, 'I'm sure the Crofts wouldn't have objected to you jumping off the end of it.'

'Last time, Mrs Ware, I believe you told me I'd be allowed on the Turbo if I got permission first from social services.'

'And that's what I still tell you.'

'You're quite serious that you'd send me through the entire bureaucracy of Brighton for five minutes of fun.'

'Mr Church,' Mandy said, as they stepped aside to let a woman pass with her baby stroller, 'tell me why you think they have a big sign right in front of the ride saying no one with a disability can go on it. No one with a back problem. No one who's pregnant, and no one with a heart condition.'

'None of which applies to me, Mrs Ware.'

'But all of which will apply,' Colin said, 'with one exception, by the time you get off.'

Mr Church walked on ahead of them. 'And you needn't treat me to a ride on the Cup and Saucer this time to assuage your conscience, Mrs Ware,' he called back, rejoining the others.

It was a second or two later that Mandy stopped and put her hand on Colin's arm. 'Wait a minute.'

'What.'

'Come back here a minute.' She returned a little way toward a souvenir shop they'd passed while they were talking to Mr Church. 'What about him.' Mandy pointed to the man in the shop.

Colin looked at him through an open window as he tied a balloon up to the ceiling.

'There's plenty of light in there. You can really see him well. He's standing pretty still.'

Colin continued looking through the window at him.

'I'm sure you could draw him, Colin.'

'Possibly.'

'Will you try?'

The man reached through the window to rearrange several plastic fish on the shelf outside.

'Go get your things,' she said. 'Just let me know where you park, and I'll take everyone back.'

The man glanced up at them. Colin nodded to him.

'You'll have all the time you want.'

'Possibly,' Colin said again, studying the man.

'Because you really do have to get back to work, Colin. Jeremy told me that's really, really important.'

'I'll see what he says,' Colin said, starting toward the shopkeeper.

By the time Colin had returned with his art materials, the others were finished at the end of the pier and had gathered at the photography stand Mrs Campbell had noticed on their last visit. There was a large painted board with two figures on it, one of them a mermaid lying on a rock, and beside her a deep-sea diver emerging from the ocean. But instead of faces, two oval holes had been cut in the board, and looking out through the hole for the mermaid's face was Mrs Campbell, the mermaid's long blond hair flowing down over her bare shoulders to partially cover her breasts.

They were farther on down the pier, so they didn't see Colin as he stopped, watching as Mandy tried to persuade one of the men to put his face into the opening beside Mrs Campbell's, then finally going around to the other side of the board herself to put her own face into the opening for the deep-sea diver, so the photographer could click the picture. Then the seven of them continued on along the pier toward him.

'You have your set of van keys then,' Colin said, as she reached them, 'and you can get along without me for a bit.'

She kissed him on the cheek. 'Just draw, Colin.'

There were windows on all sides of the souvenir shop, so after he'd tried and failed to draw the shopkeeper from one angle, Colin was able to go around and attempt to portray him from another.

But after tearing up the second attempt he decided not to waste another sheet of paper and closed his pad.

The man came out of the shop carrying a shirt on a hanger. 'How's it going.'

'I'm done.'

'Do I get to see it?' He hung the blue-and-white striped shirt on a nail beside the door.

'It didn't work out. I apologise for taking up your time.'

The man turned around to watch Colin putting his pencils back in his case. 'Why didn't it work out.'

'I couldn't say.' Colin snapped shut the clasp. 'I wish I knew myself.' He lowered the case to his side.

'I wouldn't worry about it.'

'I am worried about it. I'm very worried about it.'

'We all have our bad days,' the man said.

'Try bad months.'

The two of them stood looking at each other a few moments.

'Are you visiting Brighton?'

'I live here now. Since November.'

'And before that?'

'London.'

The shopkeeper began straightening a row of small rubber figures on the shelf. 'Maybe you miss the urban rhythms. My sister and her husband saved up twenty years for a cottage down in Cornwall. Finally moved there, got so bored they were back before the month was up and haven't left the city since.'

'It's not that.'

'You're sure.'

'A couple of mornings I've taken the train up to London. I tried to get working again by going around the old places. I hoped the associations would trigger something.'

'No good?'

'Nothing.'

The man picked up one of the rubber figures, which was a sunbather in a beach chair. 'Look at this shit they send you now.' He showed Colin where one of the figure's legs was hanging partially off.

'My inspiration,' Colin said. 'It's just gone.'

'Globalisation. That's what this is all about. They never sent me shit like this before globalisation.'

'I've lost my art.'

The man shook the figure, then took hold of its leg and twisted it till it came off.

'Jesus Christ, I've lost my art and I don't know what to do.'

'The global village,' the man said, reaching into his booth to drop the figure and its leg into a wastebasket. 'That's where your global village belongs.'

'I've lost my very essence.'

'No you haven't.'

'I have. Don't tell me I haven't.'

'It'll come back.'

'I heard about a woman who lost her religion,' Colin said, looking off across the sea. 'This is the same.'

'What happened to her.'

'She tore all her hair out and they had to lock her up.'

'Why don't you take a few deep breaths.'

'I'm realising the most terrible thing an artist can realise about himself,' Colin said, looking up at him again. 'My wife and I are in charge of some pensioners. I haven't told this to anyone before, but sometimes I'll get in a panic and go in and try to draw them while they're asleep. Or through the window when they're out on the lawn. Or from behind without them seeing me. I've been leading a secret life, the life of someone slowly losing their sanity.'

'Aren't there any johns on this pier?'

They turned to see a woman standing beside them holding her bag.

'What do you have to do for a john around here,' she said.

The man glanced at Colin.

'A john,' Colin said. 'Yes. Well I think there's one back in the arcade.'

'Where?'

Colin pointed. 'The big building with all the games in it.'

There was another tourist coming toward them with a large leather case on a strap over his shoulder. 'He says there's one where the games are,' she yelled at him. She looked back at Colin. 'I didn't see one in there.'

'I think you have to ask for the key at the snack bar.'

'He thinks you have to ask for the key at the snack bar,' she said to her husband, as he approached.

'Well get your butt back there and ask for it then.'

'What are you going to do,' she said, as he stopped next to them.

'Wait here for you.'

She looked toward the front of the pier for a moment, then back at her husband. 'What time is it.'

'Look at your own watch.'

'I didn't change it for here yet.'

The man unslung his case from over his shoulder and set it on the pier, then pushed the sleeve of his shirt up enough to see his watch. 'Quarter of three.'

'Write it down,' she said, starting away.

'You can't write it down this time?'

As the woman hurried back toward the arcade, the man bent down to unzip a compartment of his case and remove a small pad of paper. He felt the pocket of his shirt, then looked over at the shelf beside them where several pens were lined up. 'You don't mind if I borrow this,' he said, picking one up. He scribbled on the back of the pad with it till the ink began flowing. 'What day of the month is it.'

'Tenth,' the shopkeeper said.

'That's right, I knew that.'

Colin and the shopkeeper watched as he wrote in the pad.

'Write down every time the wife does a damn bowel movement,' he said. 'What the hell kind of a vacation is this.' When he finished writing he held up the pen to look at it. 'What do we have here now,' he said.

'A souvenir pen, sir.'

'What's the picture on it.'

'The Pavilion, sir.'

'The Taj Mahal or something?'

'The Pavilion here in Brighton.'

'How much,' he said, reaching into his pocket.

'One pound fifty.'

'She's got that trick bowel,' he said to Colin, pulling out a fistful of change. 'They chopped three feet out of her small intestine last summer.' He opened his hand in front of the shopkeeper.

'I'm sorry to hear it,' Colin said.

'The hell of it is there was no need for the damn operation in the first place.' He continued holding his open hand in front of the souvenir-shop owner. 'Take what you need, man, don't just stand there staring at it.'

'Yes, thank you.'

'Purely precautionary,' he said to Colin as the man picked through the coins in his hand. 'I said, "Jean, leave the damn intestine alone till they see an actual spot on it. They told you they'll see a spot on it in plenty of time."'

'Thank you.' The man stepped into his booth to put away the change.

'"I want peace of mind", she tells me. "I don't want to be worrying about going in for a scan every six months."' He returned the rest of the money to his pocket. 'You call this peace of mind? Our lives revolving around your damn "bm"s?' He touched Colin's shoulder. 'Listen to this – where was it.' He frowned. 'Tivoli Gardens, one of those. She goes in the damn john. "Write down my time," she says. There I am, sitting in the outdoor café trying to have a nice cappuccino or whatever. Gorgeous place. Just breathtaking. Trees. Jesus. "Write it down," she's squawking at me. "And this time don't forget to put how long since my last meal."' He shook his head. 'Anyway, five minutes later out she comes again. "Tear out the page. Just gas".' He reached up to feel the material of the shirt the man had hung on the nail. 'What's this, a special shirt or something?'

'Those are the Seagulls' colours,' Colin said.

'The what?'

'The colours of the Brighton side,' the shopkeeper said.

'Side?'

'Team,' Colin said.

'Oh, soccer?' He took the hanger off the nail. 'The local soccer team.' He frowned at the inside of the collar. 'Large, that should be right.' He removed the shirt from the hanger, quickly took off his own shirt and handed it to Colin while he pulled the striped one down over his head. 'How's this,' he said.

'A very good fit, sir.'

'Have you got a medium in there for the wife?'

'I should have,' he said, going into his small shop.

'I was in America last year myself,' Colin said, handing him back his shirt.

'Oh? What part.'

'Vermont.'

'Oh sure.'

'A town called New Cardiff.'

'What is it?'

'New Cardiff.'

The tourist shook his head. 'Can't say I've heard of it.'

'It's quite small.'

'New England. That's not really our beat. Nothing against the place.'

The shopkeeper came out carrying another blue-and-white shirt. 'My last medium,' he said.

'Good, and get one for yourself while you're at it,' the tourist said, taking it from him. 'Put it on my tab.' He bunched up the shirt he'd been wearing before, bent down and stuffed it into his case. When he straightened up the shopkeeper was still standing looking at him. 'Now what,' the tourist said.

'I didn't quite understand, sir.'

'Get yourself a shirt.'

'A shirt?'

'Like mine.'

'For myself?'

The tourist reached over to pull slightly at the front of the man's sweater. 'I catch any of my people out on the floor in a ratty old thing like this,' he said, grinning over at Colin, 'they've got a broom in their hand and they're back at square one.' He looked back at the shopkeeper. 'Are you running this place to make money or what. Get one of these nice shirts on yourself.'

The man turned around and went into his shop again.

'How about one for you,' the tourist said to Colin.

'I'm Fulham.'

'You're what?'

'Listen,' Colin said, 'I'm thinking of something.'

The man glanced down at the shelf coming out below the window of the store. 'Look at this.' He motioned for Colin to step over beside him. 'Look here.'

'What's that,' Colin said, looking down at the rows of souvenirs on the shelf.

'First of all,' the tourist said, picking up a cellophane-wrapped stick from the shelf, 'what in hell is he doing with his candy canes out this time of year.'

'I think that's Brighton Rock,' Colin said.

'You think it's what?'

Colin took it from him. 'That's what it is.' He unwrapped one end and showed it to him. 'The little letters going around,' he said. 'They spell "Brighton".'

The man squinted at it.

'They go all the way through,' Colin said, turning it around to show him the letters on the other end.

The man took it back, finished unwrapping it and broke it in half. 'I'll be goddamned,' he said, looking at the tiny letters on the broken ends.

'It's a tradition here.'

'What's he want for these.' The tourist picked up a sign from behind the rock. 'Will you look at this thing?' He held it up in front of Colin. 'He's got some kind of stencilled numbers on an old piece of cardboard. Christ, it looks like something left over from the last World War.' He studied the numbers. 'A pound twenty each. Then he's got five for four pounds. Where's the logic to that – this character's a real piece of work.' He returned the sign and picked out four more sticks of rock. 'I'll tell you what his problem is. Hold these.' He handed them to Colin. 'First of all, he's got his candy coming down here, then his buses.' He began exchanging the row of rock with a row of little red double-decker buses. 'Then he's got another fucking row of candy over here, separate from the first candy. Keep your candy together, man, you're scrambling up your product areas. How basic can we get.' He picked up a souvenir from another row. 'What's this now.'

'Big Ben in the snow,' Colin said.

He shook it, watching for a moment as the tiny white flakes whirled around inside the glass globe. 'I mean these things went out with the hula hoop, but if you're going to have something like this at least set up your table so your eye is drawn from item to item in a pleasing motion. The way he's got this stuff set up you go cross-eyed looking at it. Let's put these back here for him.'

Colin watched as he moved all the globes of Big Ben into a row along the back.

'I have a small favour to ask,' Colin said. 'I don't know if it's something you have time for or not.'

The man finished arranging the glass domes and stepped over beside Colin. 'Listen, I don't want to say this directly to him myself. I don't want him to take offence, but when I see a fellow man who could be doing something a little better than what he is, I always want to reach out and help – that's just the way I am.'

'What don't you want to say to him,' Colin said.

The tourist took a step closer. 'The damn guy looks like he's the head pallbearer at his best friend's funeral,' he said quietly. 'So after me and the wife move along, take him aside, one Englishman to another, and say, "Friend, I think a great big smile on that face of yours would go one heck of a long way toward pulling those customers over to your shop on their way down to the Ferris wheel." Will you tell him that for me?'

The man stepped out of the shop wearing a blue-and-white striped shirt.

'Hey. Now we're getting serious.' The tourist grinned, nodded, then turned to Colin again. 'I believe our friend's starting to get serious about doing some business around here. Am I right? Oh listen.' He bent down and opened his case. 'I've got the videocam.' He lifted it out. 'When the wife comes back I'll have her slip on her Seagull shirt and maybe you could shoot us over there by the railing. Think you can handle this thing?'

'I believe so,' Colin said, taking the camera from him. 'Maybe I could take the two of you on one of the rides. A little more action.'

'Oh I like that.' He clapped Colin on the side of the arm. 'You're my man. Let me settle up with our Salesman of the Month here first.' He removed his wallet from his rear pocket. 'We've got three shirts, five of the souvenir candies.' He took the rock from Colin to hand to the shopkeeper. 'And let's toss in a few buses while we're at it.' He reached down to scoop up some of the little red buses in his hands. 'Total us up, my good man,' he said, holding them in front of the shopkeeper. 'Oh by the way, while you were inside I cleaned up your display table for you. No charge. No charge.'

Colin bent down to set the videocam back in the man's bag. 'Before the wife gets back,' he said, straightening up and opening his drawing pad, 'there's a small favour I have to ask of you.'

* * *

354